nickelodeon

降击神通

AVATAR

THE LAST AIRBENDER

TEAM AVATAR TALES

Created by
Bryan Konietzko
Michael Dante DiMartino

Featuring the work of
Carla Speed McNeil
Coni Yovaniniz
Cris Peter
Dave Scheidt
Faith Erin Hicks
Gene Luen Yang
Sam Manley Lee
Sasaku Hughes
Mark Pien
Little Corvus
Natalie Riess
Ron Koertge
Ryan Hill
Sara Goetter

Cover by
Sara Kipin

DARK HORSE BOOKS

president and publisher
MIKE RICHARDSON

editor
RACHEL ROBERTS

assistant editor
JENNY BLENK

collection designer
SARAH TERRY

digital art technicians
CHRISTIANNE GILLENARDO-GOUDREAU
and **SAMANTHA HUMMER**

Special thanks to Linda Lee, James Salerno, and Joan Hilty at Nickelodeon,
and to Bryan Konietzko, Michael Dante DiMartino, and Tim Hedrick.

Published by **Dark Horse Books**
A division of Dark Horse Comics LLC
10956 SE Main Street, Milwaukie, OR 97222

DarkHorse.com
Nick.com

To find a comics shop in your area, visit comicshoplocator.com

First edition: October 2019 | ISBN 978-1-50670-793-8
Digital ISBN 978-1-50671-145-4

3 5 7 9 10 8 6 4
Printed in China

Neil Hankerson Executive Vice President • Tom Weddle Chief Financial Officer • Randy Stradley Vice
President of Publishing • Nick McWhorter Chief Business Development Officer • Matt Parkinson Vice
President of Marketing • Dale LaFountain Vice President of Information Technology • Cara Niece Vice
President of Production and Scheduling • Mark Bernardi Vice President of Book Trade and Digital Sales
• Ken Lizzi General Counsel • Dave Marshall Editor in Chief • Davey Estrada Editorial Director • Chris
Warner Senior Books Editor • Cary Grazzini Director of Specialty Projects • Lia Ribacchi Art Director •
Vanessa Todd-Holmes Director of Print Purchasing • Matt Dryer Director of Digital Art and Prepress •
Michael Gombos Senior Director of Licensed Publications • Kari Yadro Director of Custom Programs • Kari
Torson Director of International Licensing • Sean Brice Director of Trade Sales

CONTENTS

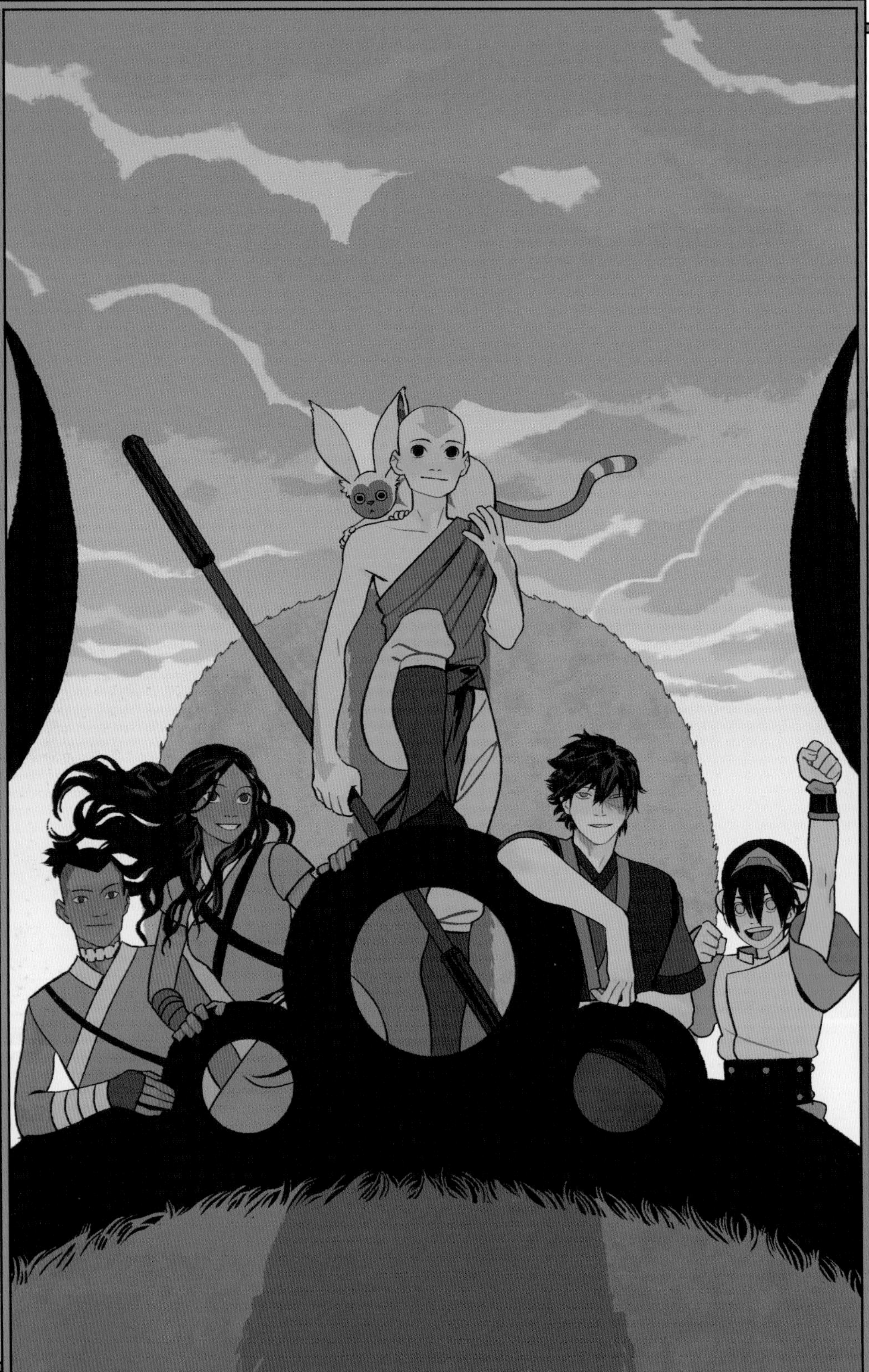

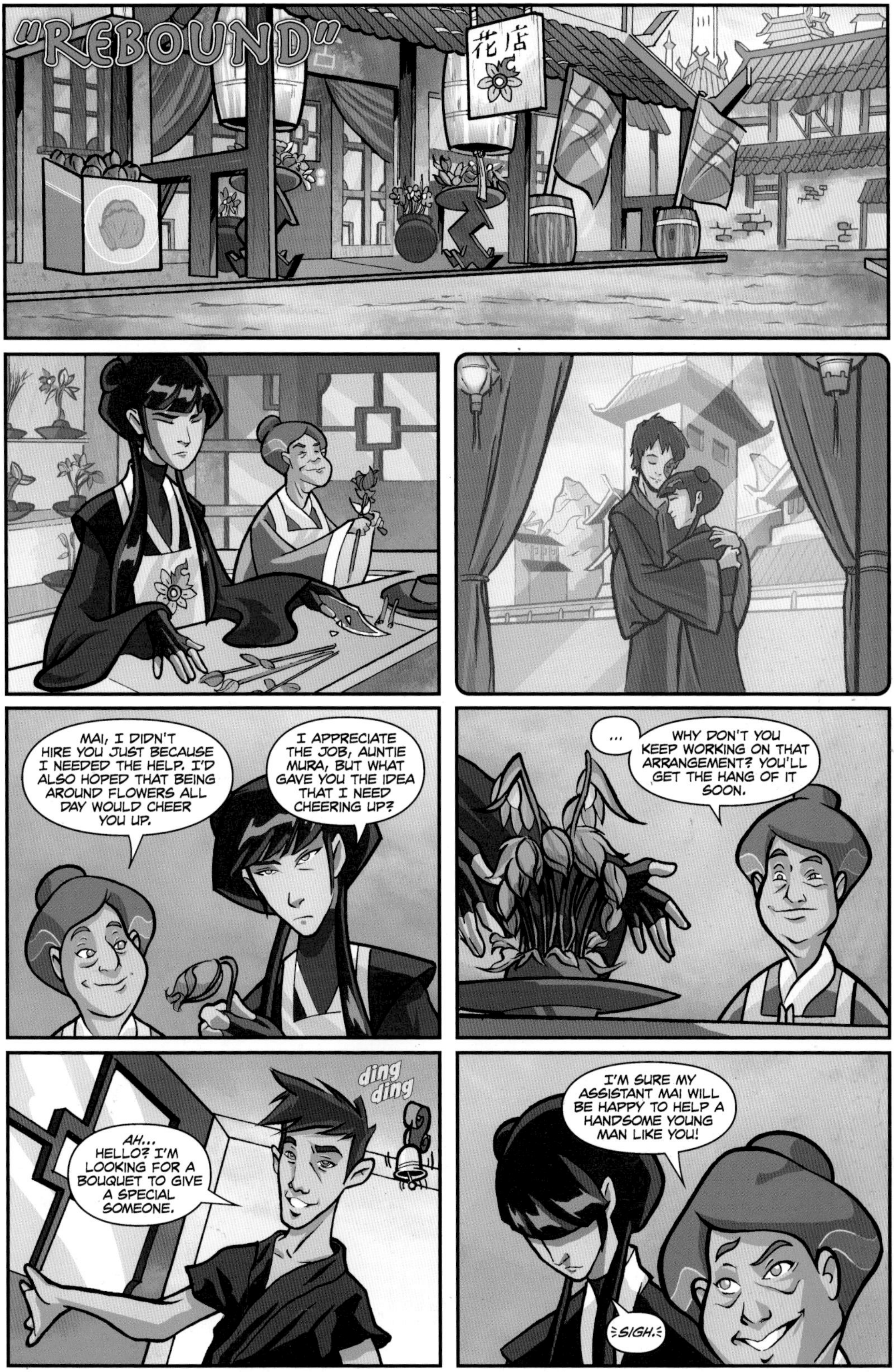
"REBOUND"
花店
MAI, I DIDN'T HIRE YOU JUST BECAUSE I NEEDED THE HELP. I'D ALSO HOPED THAT BEING AROUND FLOWERS ALL DAY WOULD CHEER YOU UP.
I APPRECIATE THE JOB, AUNTIE MURA, BUT WHAT GAVE YOU THE IDEA THAT I NEED CHEERING UP?
...
WHY DON'T YOU KEEP WORKING ON THAT ARRANGEMENT? YOU'LL GET THE HANG OF IT SOON.
ding ding
AH... HELLO? I'M LOOKING FOR A BOUQUET TO GIVE A SPECIAL SOMEONE.
I'M SURE MY ASSISTANT MAI WILL BE HAPPY TO HELP A HANDSOME YOUNG MAN LIKE YOU!
SIGH.

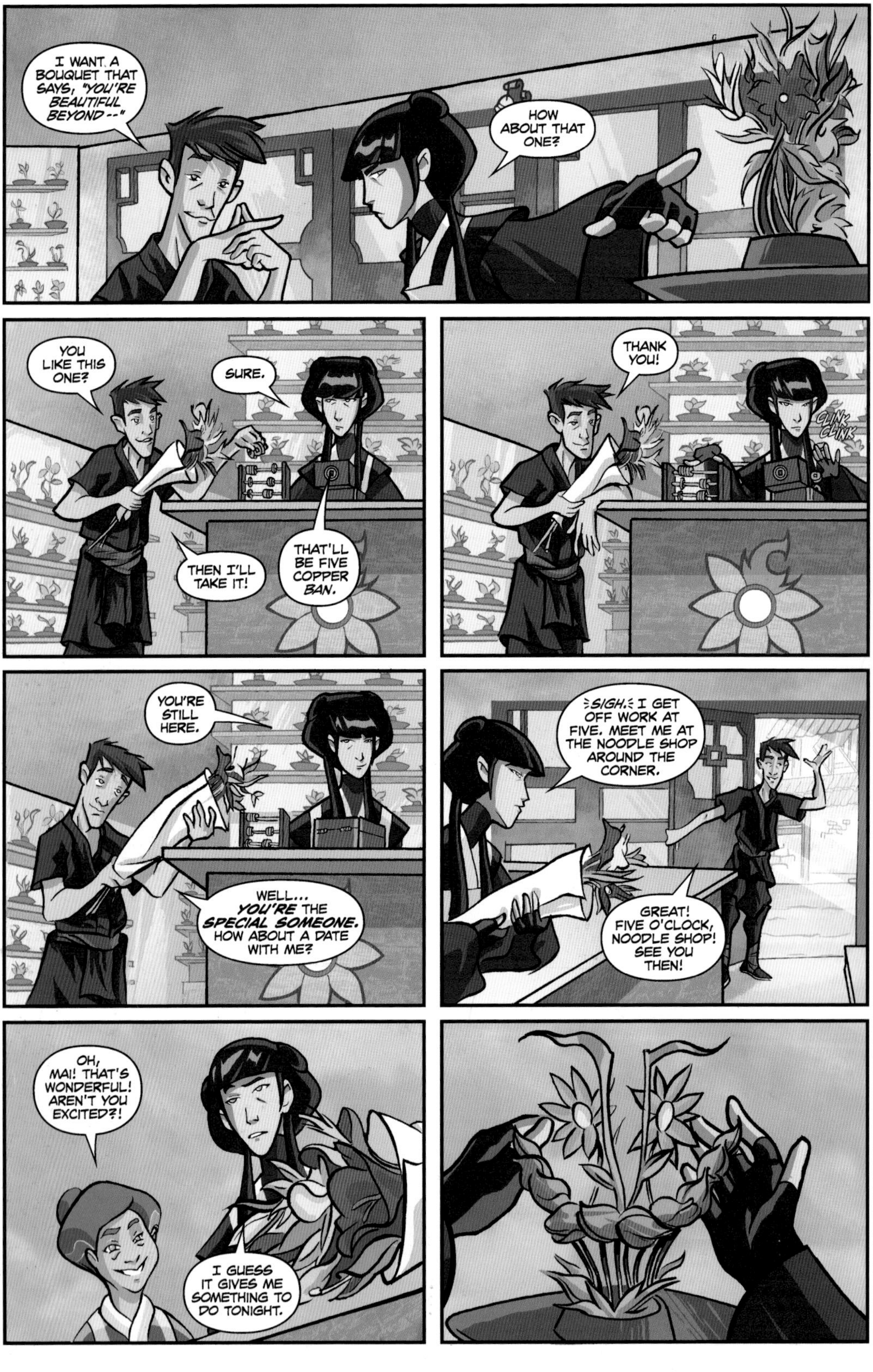
I WANT A BOUQUET THAT SAYS, "YOU'RE BEAUTIFUL BEYOND --"
HOW ABOUT THAT ONE?
YOU LIKE THIS ONE?
SURE.
THEN I'LL TAKE IT!
THAT'LL BE FIVE COPPER *BAN*.
THANK YOU!
CLINK CLINK
YOU'RE STILL HERE.
WELL... ***YOU'RE*** THE ***SPECIAL SOMEONE.*** HOW ABOUT A DATE WITH ME?
SIGH. I GET OFF WORK AT FIVE. MEET ME AT THE NOODLE SHOP AROUND THE CORNER.
GREAT! FIVE O'CLOCK, NOODLE SHOP! SEE YOU THEN!
OH, MAI! THAT'S WONDERFUL! AREN'T YOU EXCITED?!
I GUESS IT GIVES ME SOMETHING TO DO TONIGHT.

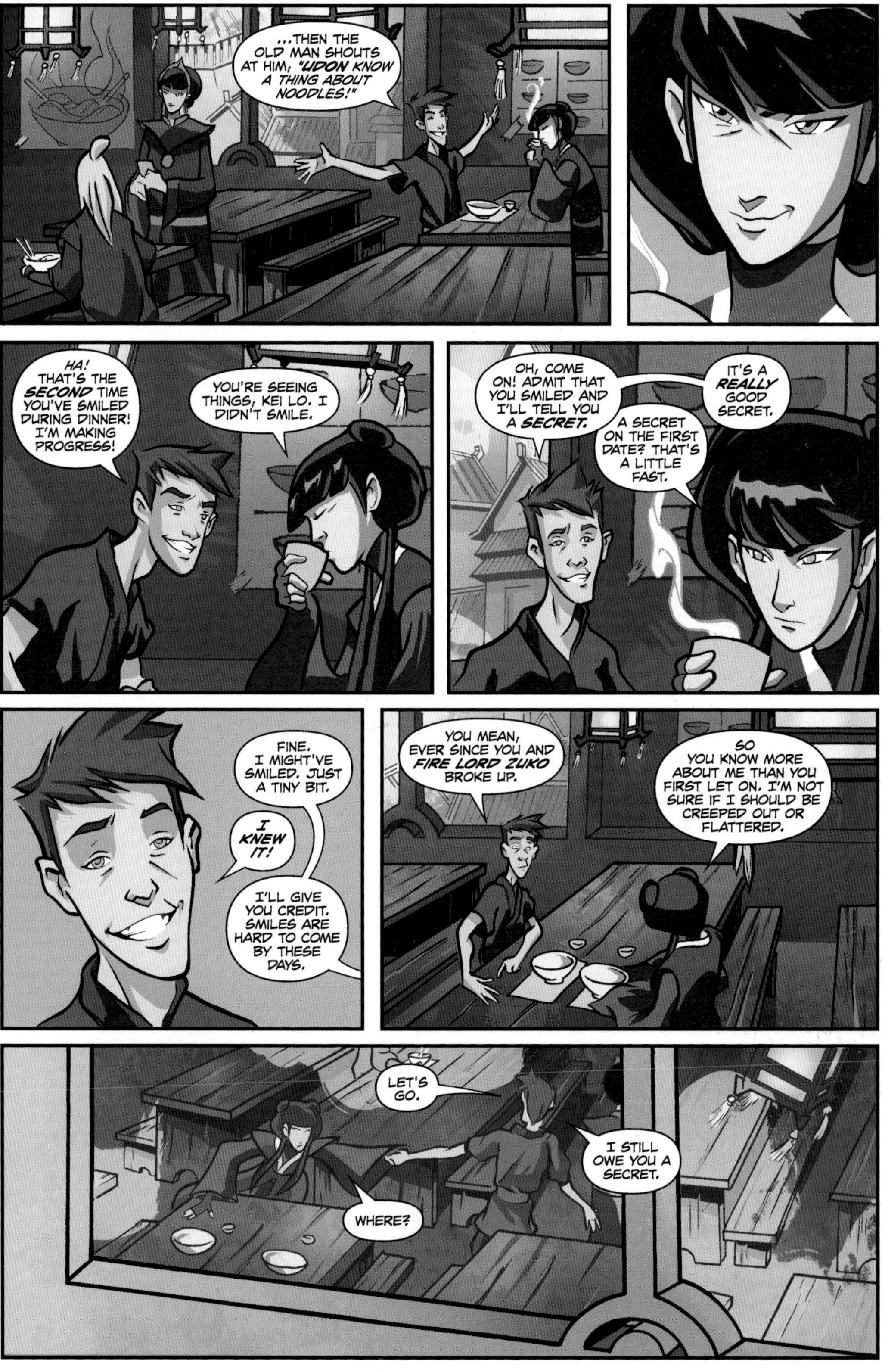
...THEN THE OLD MAN SHOUTS AT HIM, "UDON KNOW A THING ABOUT NOODLES!"
HA! THAT'S THE SECOND TIME YOU'VE SMILED DURING DINNER! I'M MAKING PROGRESS!
YOU'RE SEEING THINGS, KEI LO. I DIDN'T SMILE.
OH, COME ON! ADMIT THAT YOU SMILED AND I'LL TELL YOU A SECRET.
IT'S A REALLY GOOD SECRET.
A SECRET ON THE FIRST DATE? THAT'S A LITTLE FAST.
FINE. I MIGHT'VE SMILED. JUST A TINY BIT.
I KNEW IT!
I'LL GIVE YOU CREDIT. SMILES ARE HARD TO COME BY THESE DAYS.
YOU MEAN, EVER SINCE YOU AND FIRE LORD ZUKO BROKE UP.
SO YOU KNOW MORE ABOUT ME THAN YOU FIRST LET ON. I'M NOT SURE IF I SHOULD BE CREEPED OUT OR FLATTERED.
LET'S GO.
I STILL OWE YOU A SECRET.
WHERE?

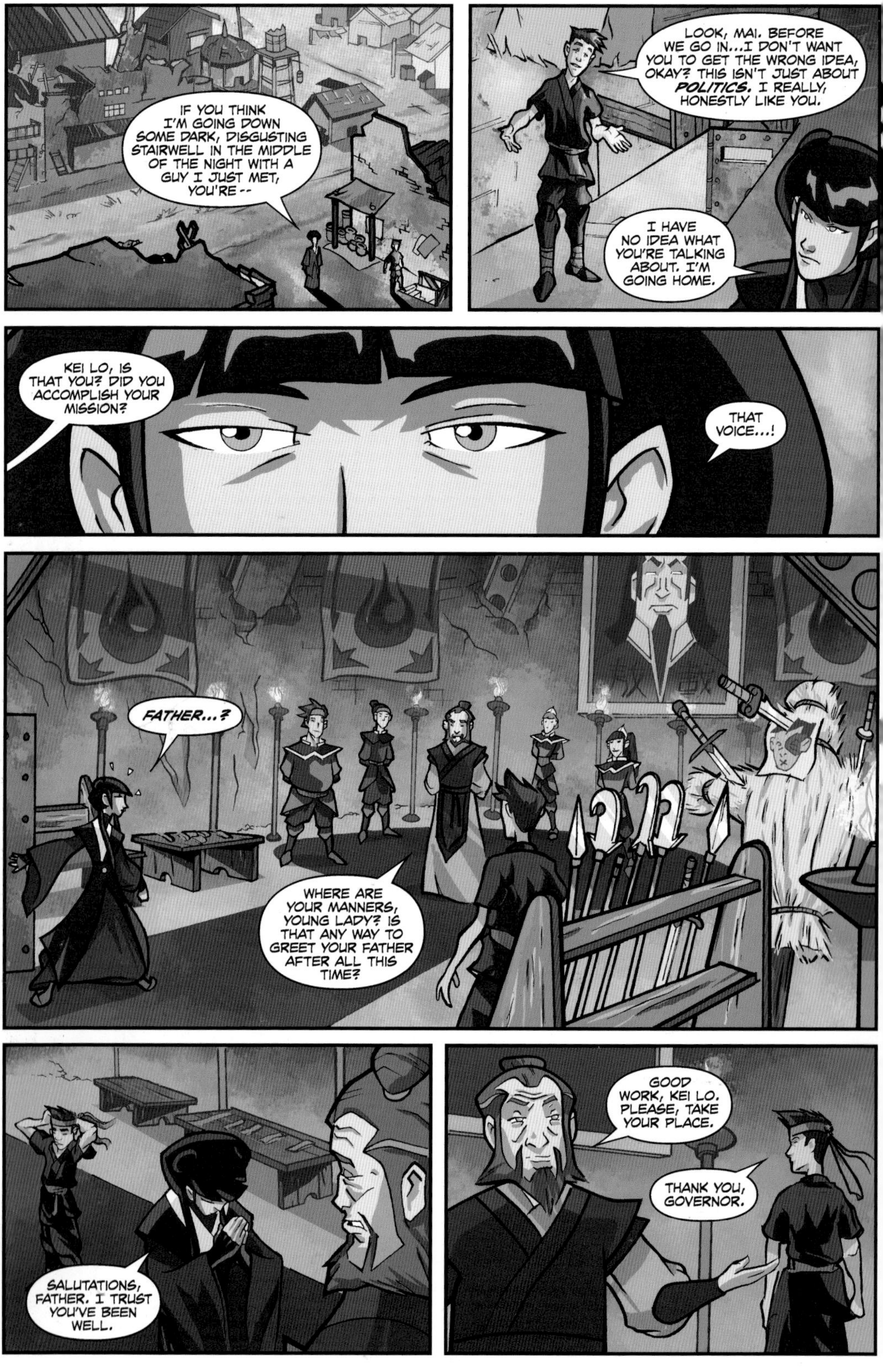
IF YOU THINK I'M GOING DOWN SOME DARK, DISGUSTING STAIRWELL IN THE MIDDLE OF THE NIGHT WITH A GUY I JUST MET, YOU'RE --
LOOK, MAI. BEFORE WE GO IN...I DON'T WANT YOU TO GET THE WRONG IDEA, OKAY? THIS ISN'T JUST ABOUT POLITICS. I REALLY, HONESTLY LIKE YOU.
I HAVE NO IDEA WHAT YOU'RE TALKING ABOUT. I'M GOING HOME.
KEI LO, IS THAT YOU? DID YOU ACCOMPLISH YOUR MISSION?
THAT VOICE...!
FATHER...?
WHERE ARE YOUR MANNERS, YOUNG LADY? IS THAT ANY WAY TO GREET YOUR FATHER AFTER ALL THIS TIME?
SALUTATIONS, FATHER. I TRUST YOU'VE BEEN WELL.
GOOD WORK, KEI LO. PLEASE, TAKE YOUR PLACE.
THANK YOU, GOVERNOR.

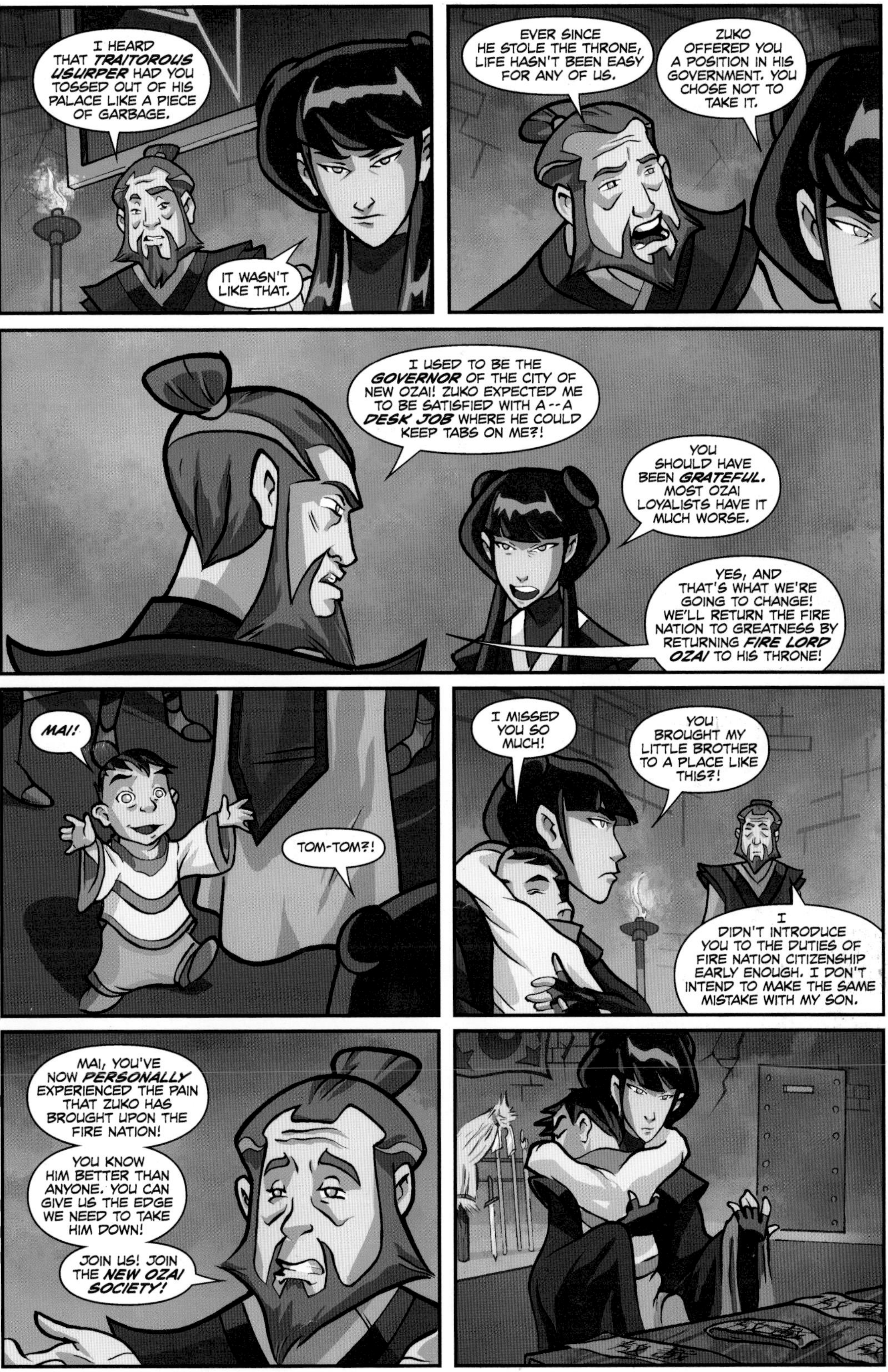

I HEARD THAT TRAITOROUS USURPER HAD YOU TOSSED OUT OF HIS PALACE LIKE A PIECE OF GARBAGE.
IT WASN'T LIKE THAT.
EVER SINCE HE STOLE THE THRONE, LIFE HASN'T BEEN EASY FOR ANY OF US.
ZUKO OFFERED YOU A POSITION IN HIS GOVERNMENT. YOU CHOSE NOT TO TAKE IT.
I USED TO BE THE GOVERNOR OF THE CITY OF NEW OZAI! ZUKO EXPECTED ME TO BE SATISFIED WITH A--A DESK JOB WHERE HE COULD KEEP TABS ON ME?!
YOU SHOULD HAVE BEEN GRATEFUL. MOST OZAI LOYALISTS HAVE IT MUCH WORSE.
YES, AND THAT'S WHAT WE'RE GOING TO CHANGE! WE'LL RETURN THE FIRE NATION TO GREATNESS BY RETURNING FIRE LORD OZAI TO HIS THRONE!
MAI!
TOM-TOM?!
I MISSED YOU SO MUCH!
YOU BROUGHT MY LITTLE BROTHER TO A PLACE LIKE THIS?!
I DIDN'T INTRODUCE YOU TO THE DUTIES OF FIRE NATION CITIZENSHIP EARLY ENOUGH. I DON'T INTEND TO MAKE THE SAME MISTAKE WITH MY SON.
MAI, YOU'VE NOW PERSONALLY EXPERIENCED THE PAIN THAT ZUKO HAS BROUGHT UPON THE FIRE NATION!
YOU KNOW HIM BETTER THAN ANYONE. YOU CAN GIVE US THE EDGE WE NEED TO TAKE HIM DOWN!
JOIN US! JOIN THE NEW OZAI SOCIETY!

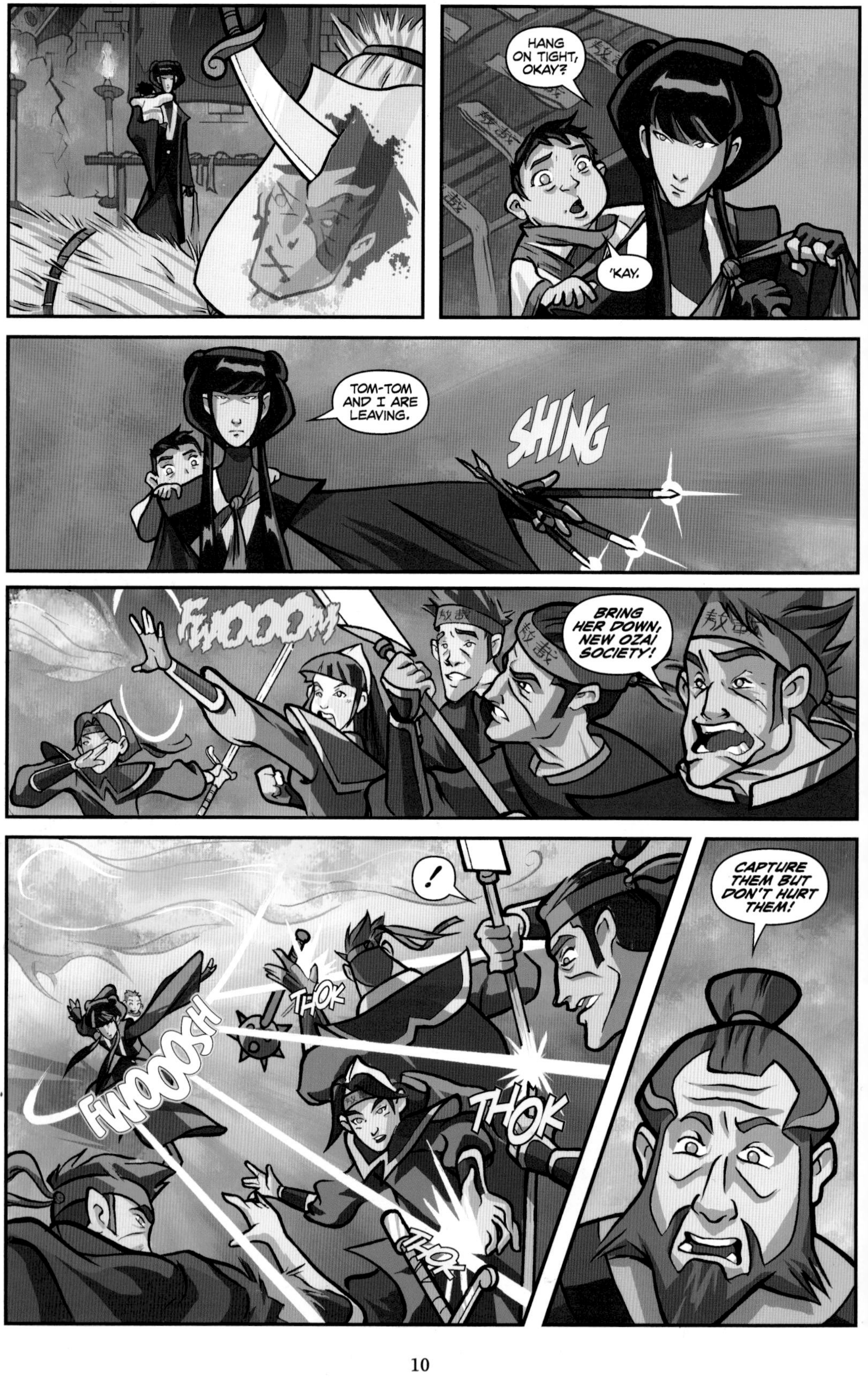
HANG ON TIGHT, OKAY?
'KAY.
TOM-TOM AND I ARE LEAVING.
SHING
FWOOOM
BRING HER DOWN, NEW OZAI SOCIETY!
!
THOK
THOK
THOK
CAPTURE THEM BUT DON'T HURT THEM!

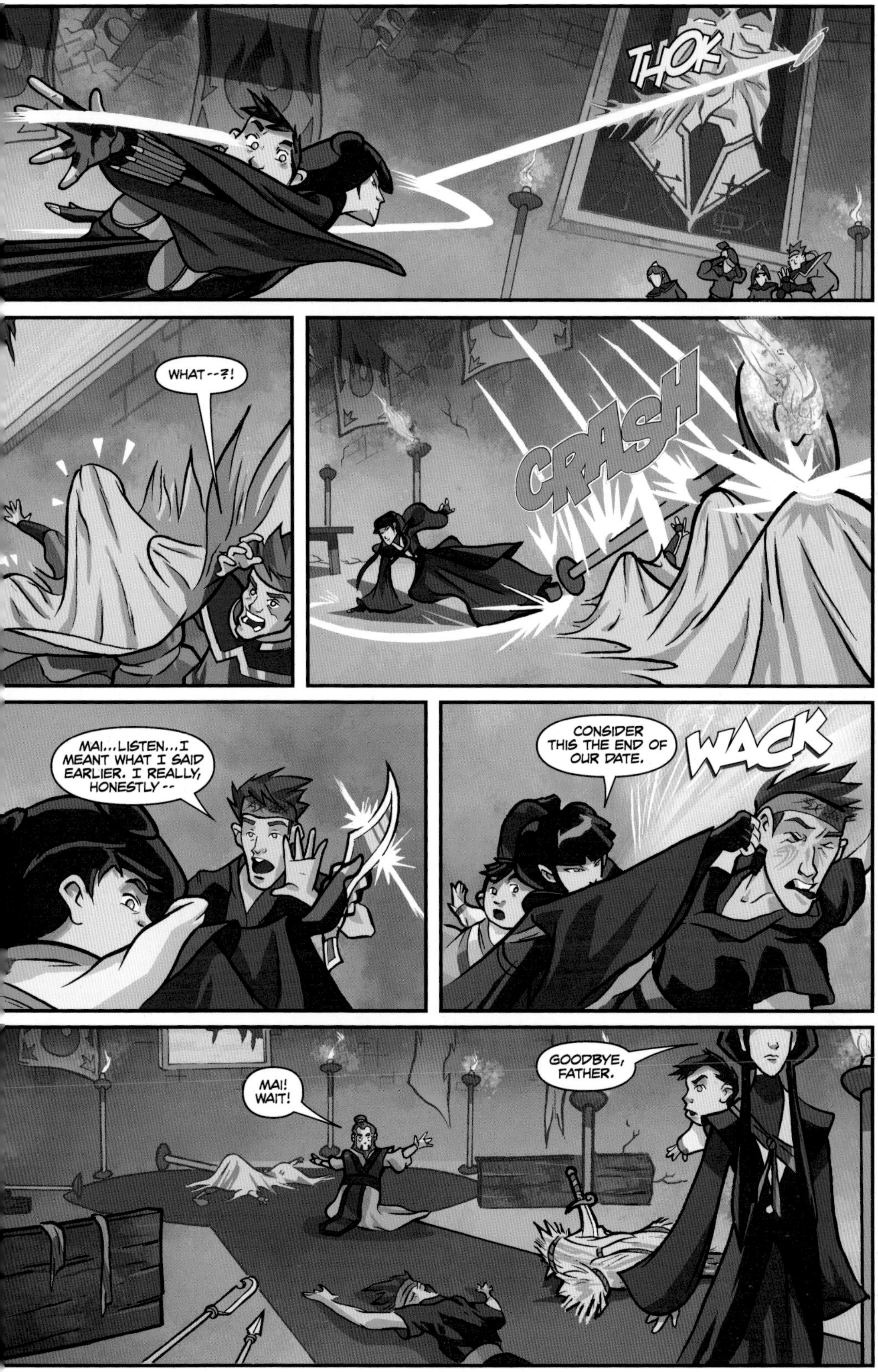
THOK
WHAT--?!
CRASH
MAI...LISTEN...I MEANT WHAT I SAID EARLIER. I REALLY, HONESTLY--
CONSIDER THIS THE END OF OUR DATE.
WACK
MAI! WAIT!
GOODBYE, FATHER.

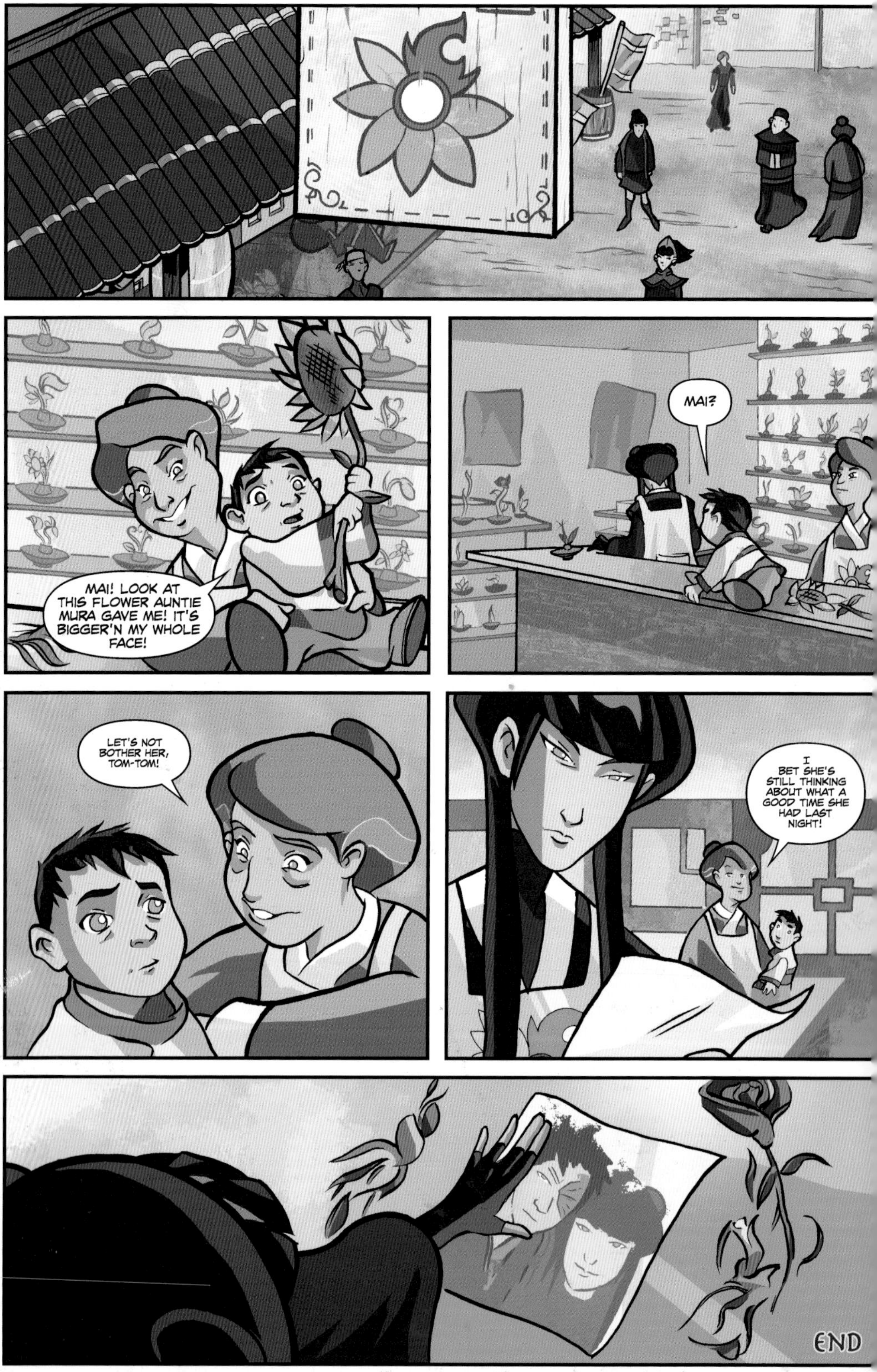
MAI! LOOK AT THIS FLOWER AUNTIE MURA GAVE ME! IT'S BIGGER'N MY WHOLE FACE!
MAI?
LET'S NOT BOTHER HER, TOM-TOM!
I BET SHE'S STILL THINKING ABOUT WHAT A GOOD TIME SHE HAD LAST NIGHT!
END

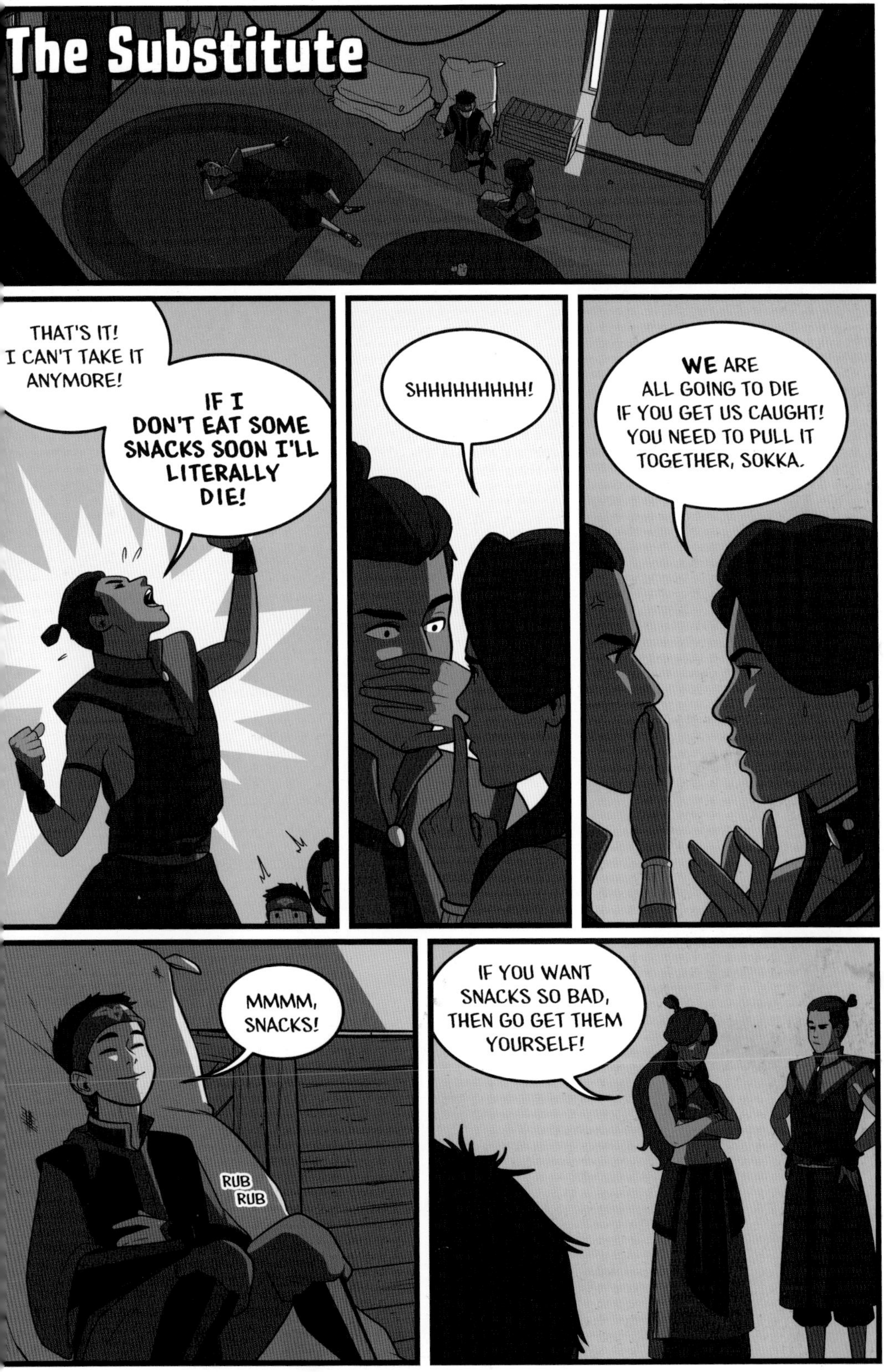
The Substitute
THAT'S IT! I CAN'T TAKE IT ANYMORE!
IF I DON'T EAT SOME SNACKS SOON I'LL LITERALLY DIE!
SHHHHHHHHH!
WE ARE ALL GOING TO DIE IF YOU GET US CAUGHT! YOU NEED TO PULL IT TOGETHER, SOKKA.
MMMM, SNACKS!
RUB RUB
IF YOU WANT SNACKS SO BAD, THEN GO GET THEM YOURSELF!

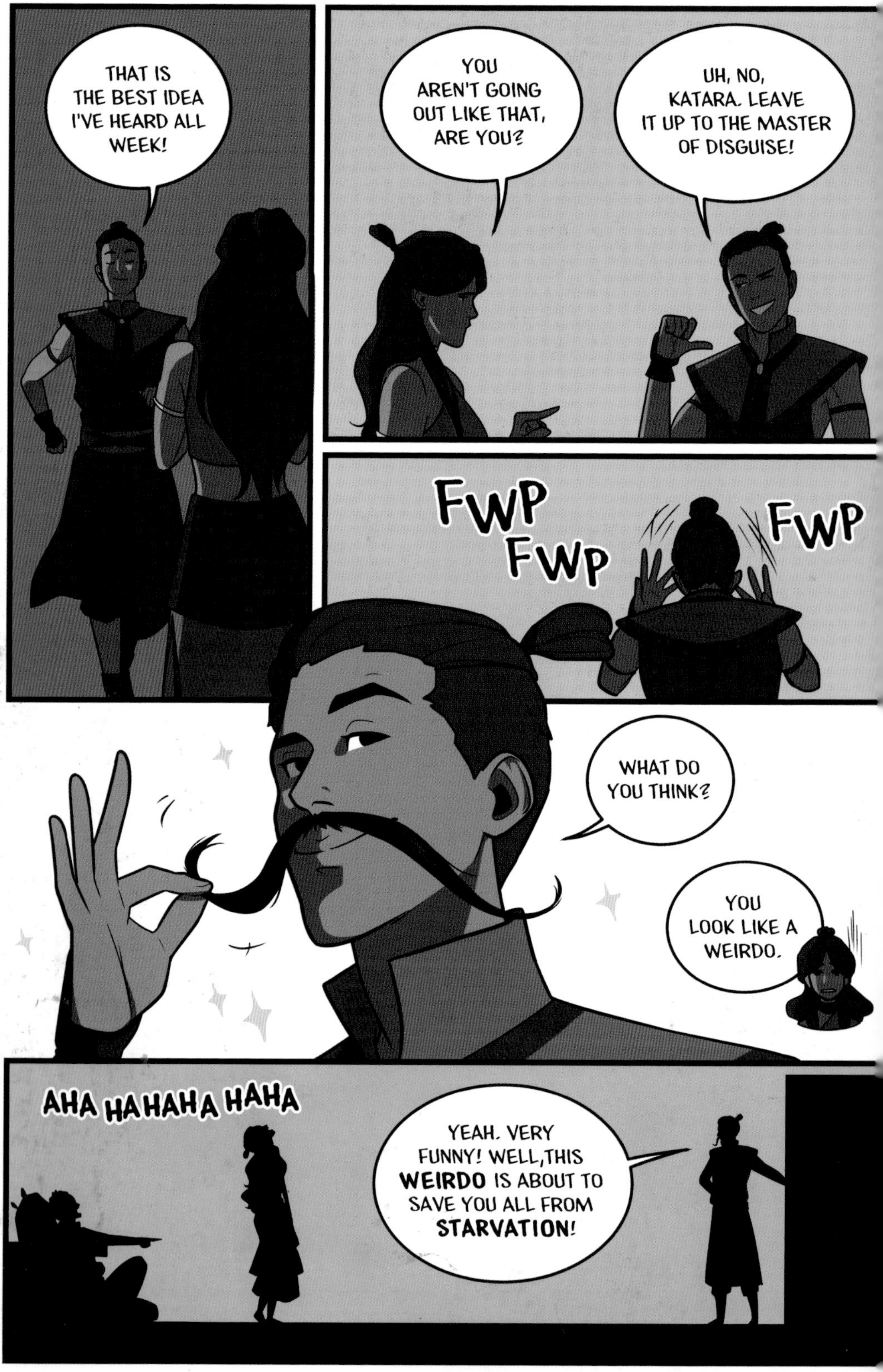
THAT IS THE BEST IDEA I'VE HEARD ALL WEEK!
YOU AREN'T GOING OUT LIKE THAT, ARE YOU?
UH, NO, KATARA. LEAVE IT UP TO THE MASTER OF DISGUISE!
FWP FWP
FWP
WHAT DO YOU THINK?
YOU LOOK LIKE A WEIRDO.
AHA HAHAHA HAHA
YEAH. VERY FUNNY! WELL, THIS WEIRDO IS ABOUT TO SAVE YOU ALL FROM STARVATION!

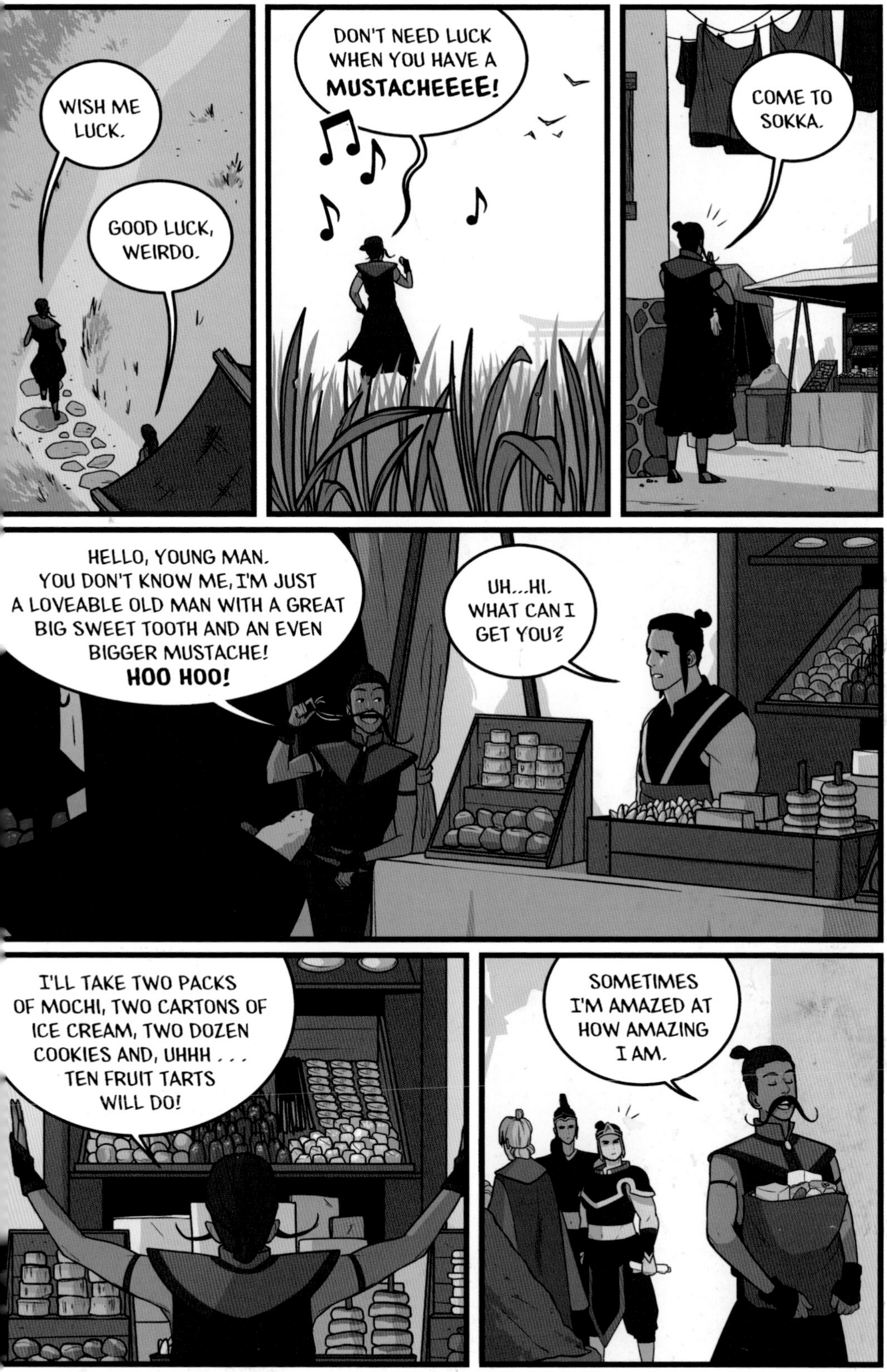

WISH ME LUCK.
GOOD LUCK, WEIRDO.
DON'T NEED LUCK WHEN YOU HAVE A MUSTACHEEEE!
COME TO SOKKA.
HELLO, YOUNG MAN. YOU DON'T KNOW ME, I'M JUST A LOVEABLE OLD MAN WITH A GREAT BIG SWEET TOOTH AND AN EVEN BIGGER MUSTACHE! HOO HOO!
UH...HI. WHAT CAN I GET YOU?
I'LL TAKE TWO PACKS OF MOCHI, TWO CARTONS OF ICE CREAM, TWO DOZEN COOKIES AND, UHHH . . . TEN FRUIT TARTS WILL DO!
SOMETIMES I'M AMAZED AT HOW AMAZING I AM.

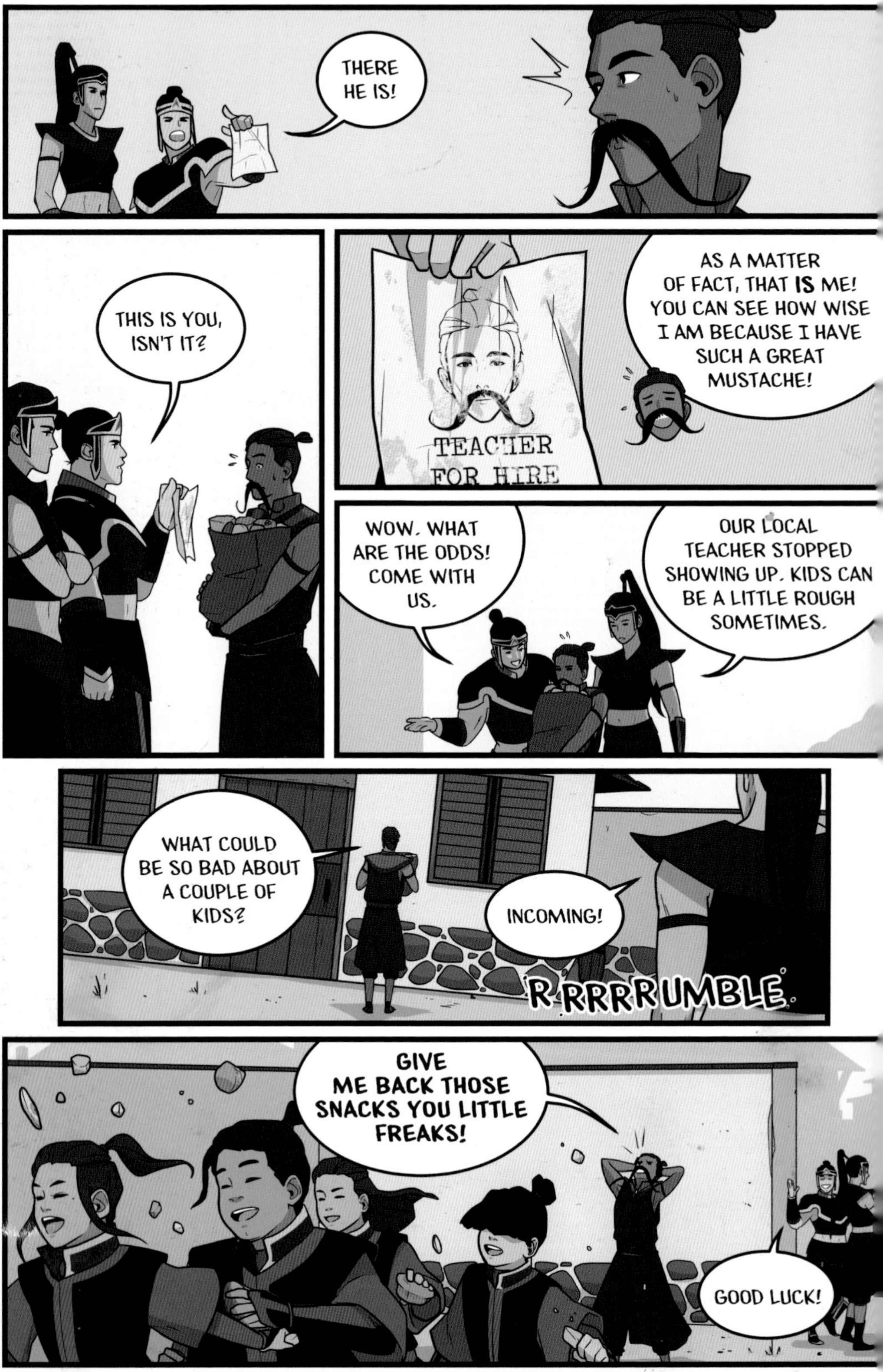
THERE HE IS!
THIS IS YOU, ISN'T IT?
TEACHER FOR HIRE
AS A MATTER OF FACT, THAT IS ME! YOU CAN SEE HOW WISE I AM BECAUSE I HAVE SUCH A GREAT MUSTACHE!
WOW. WHAT ARE THE ODDS! COME WITH US.
OUR LOCAL TEACHER STOPPED SHOWING UP. KIDS CAN BE A LITTLE ROUGH SOMETIMES.
WHAT COULD BE SO BAD ABOUT A COUPLE OF KIDS?
INCOMING!
RRRRRUMBLE
GIVE ME BACK THOSE SNACKS YOU LITTLE FREAKS!
GOOD LUCK!

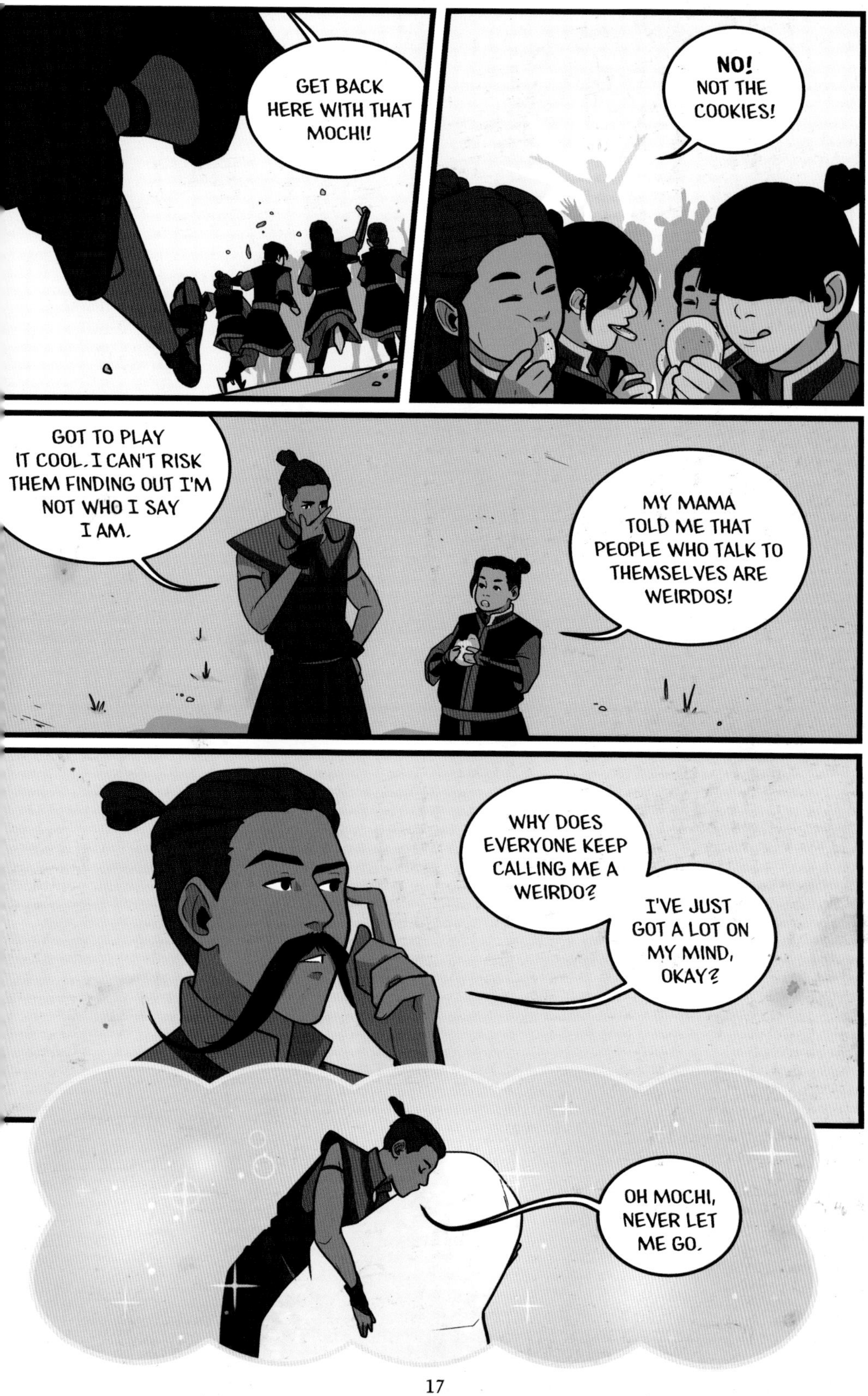
GET BACK HERE WITH THAT MOCHI!
NO! NOT THE COOKIES!
GOT TO PLAY IT COOL. I CAN'T RISK THEM FINDING OUT I'M NOT WHO I SAY I AM.
MY MAMA TOLD ME THAT PEOPLE WHO TALK TO THEMSELVES ARE WEIRDOS!
WHY DOES EVERYONE KEEP CALLING ME A WEIRDO?
I'VE JUST GOT A LOT ON MY MIND, OKAY?
OH MOCHI, NEVER LET ME GO.

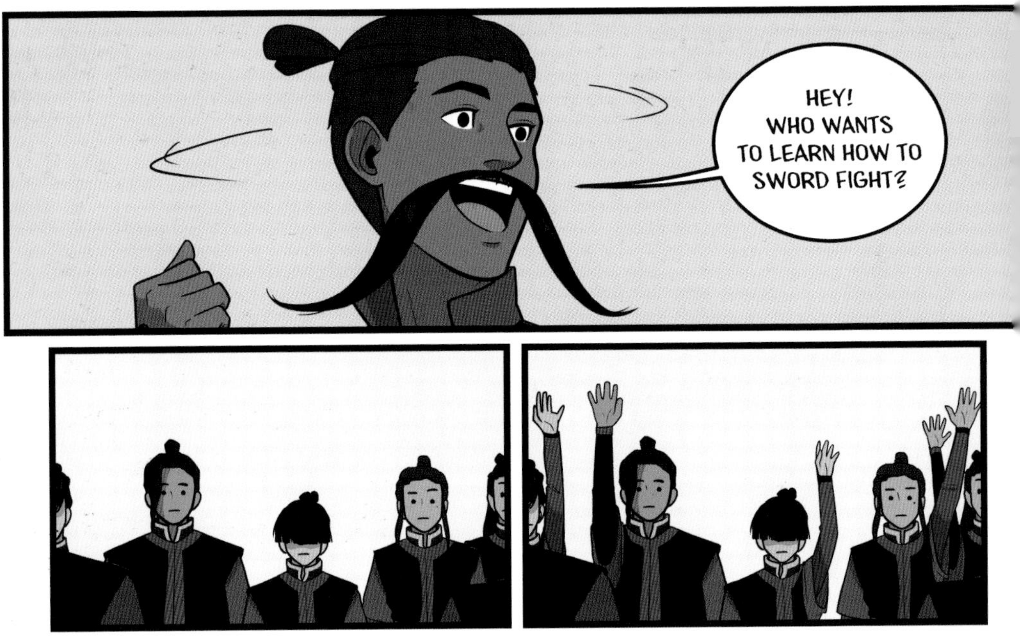
HEY!
WHO WANTS
TO LEARN HOW TO
SWORD FIGHT?

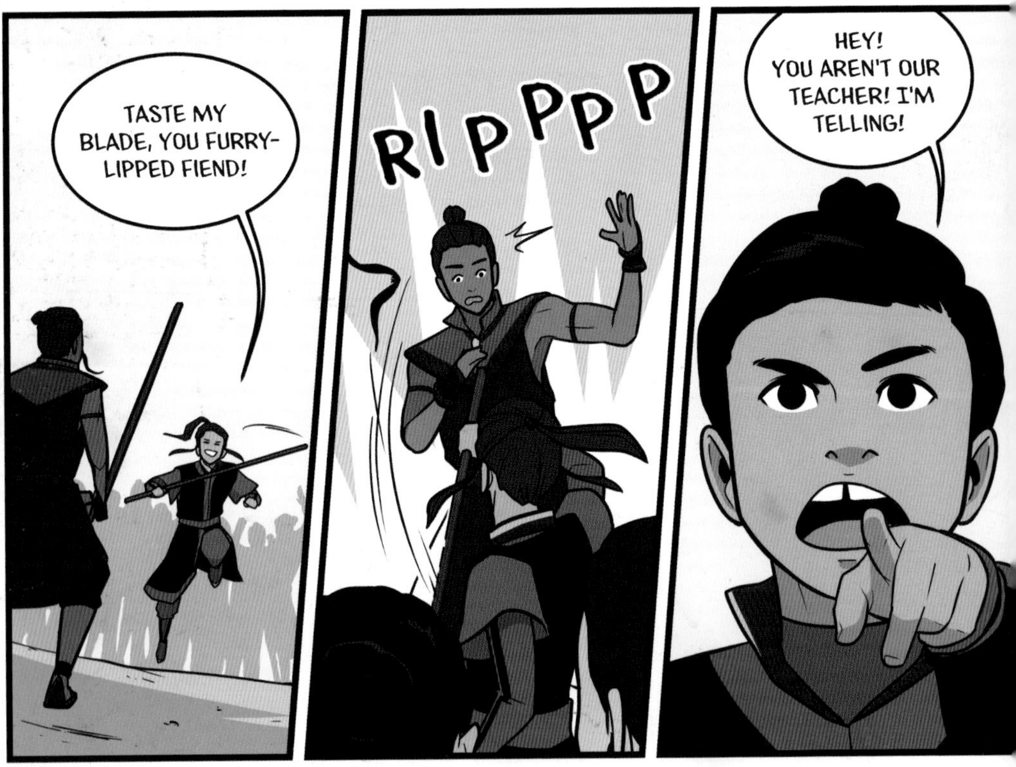
TASTE MY
BLADE, YOU FURRY-
LIPPED FIEND!
RIPPPP
HEY!
YOU AREN'T OUR
TEACHER! I'M
TELLING!

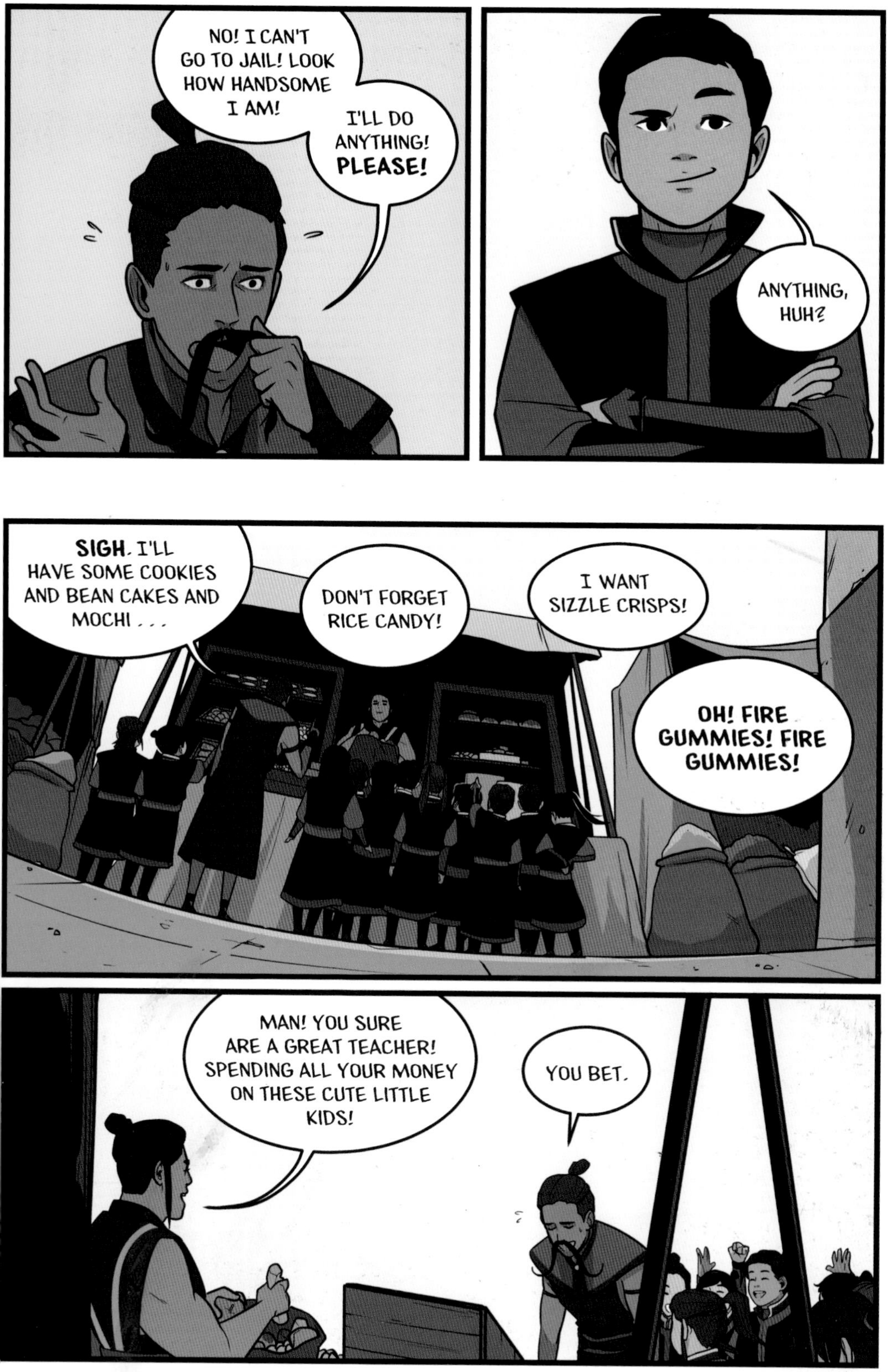
NO! I CAN'T GO TO JAIL! LOOK HOW HANDSOME I AM!
I'LL DO ANYTHING! PLEASE!
ANYTHING, HUH?
SIGH. I'LL HAVE SOME COOKIES AND BEAN CAKES AND MOCHI . . .
DON'T FORGET RICE CANDY!
I WANT SIZZLE CRISPS!
OH! FIRE GUMMIES! FIRE GUMMIES!
MAN! YOU SURE ARE A GREAT TEACHER! SPENDING ALL YOUR MONEY ON THESE CUTE LITTLE KIDS!
YOU BET.

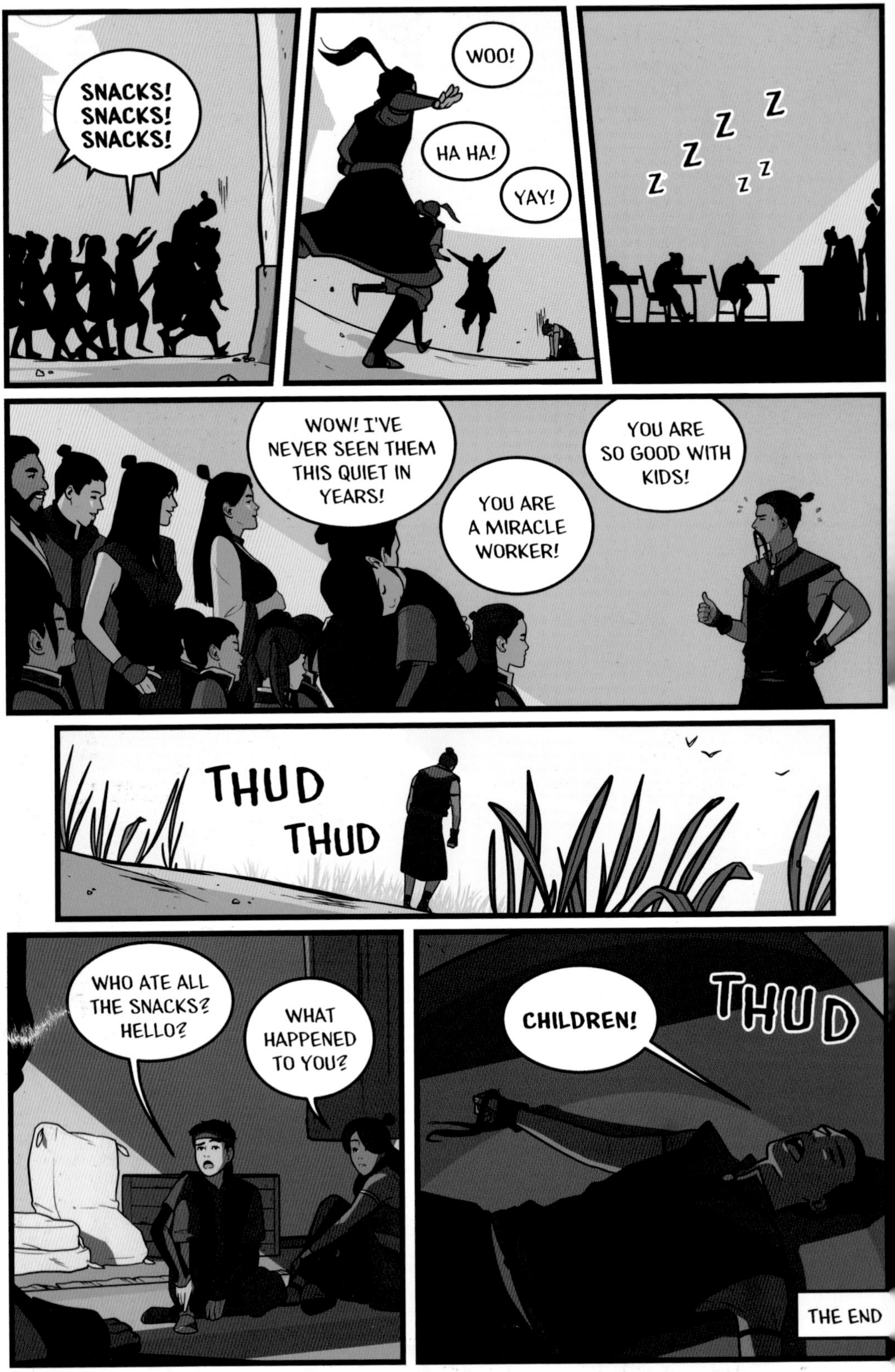
SNACKS! SNACKS! SNACKS!
WOO!
HA HA!
YAY!
Z Z Z Z
Z Z
WOW! I'VE NEVER SEEN THEM THIS QUIET IN YEARS!
YOU ARE A MIRACLE WORKER!
YOU ARE SO GOOD WITH KIDS!
THUD
THUD
WHO ATE ALL THE SNACKS? HELLO?
WHAT HAPPENED TO YOU?
CHILDREN!
THUD
THE END

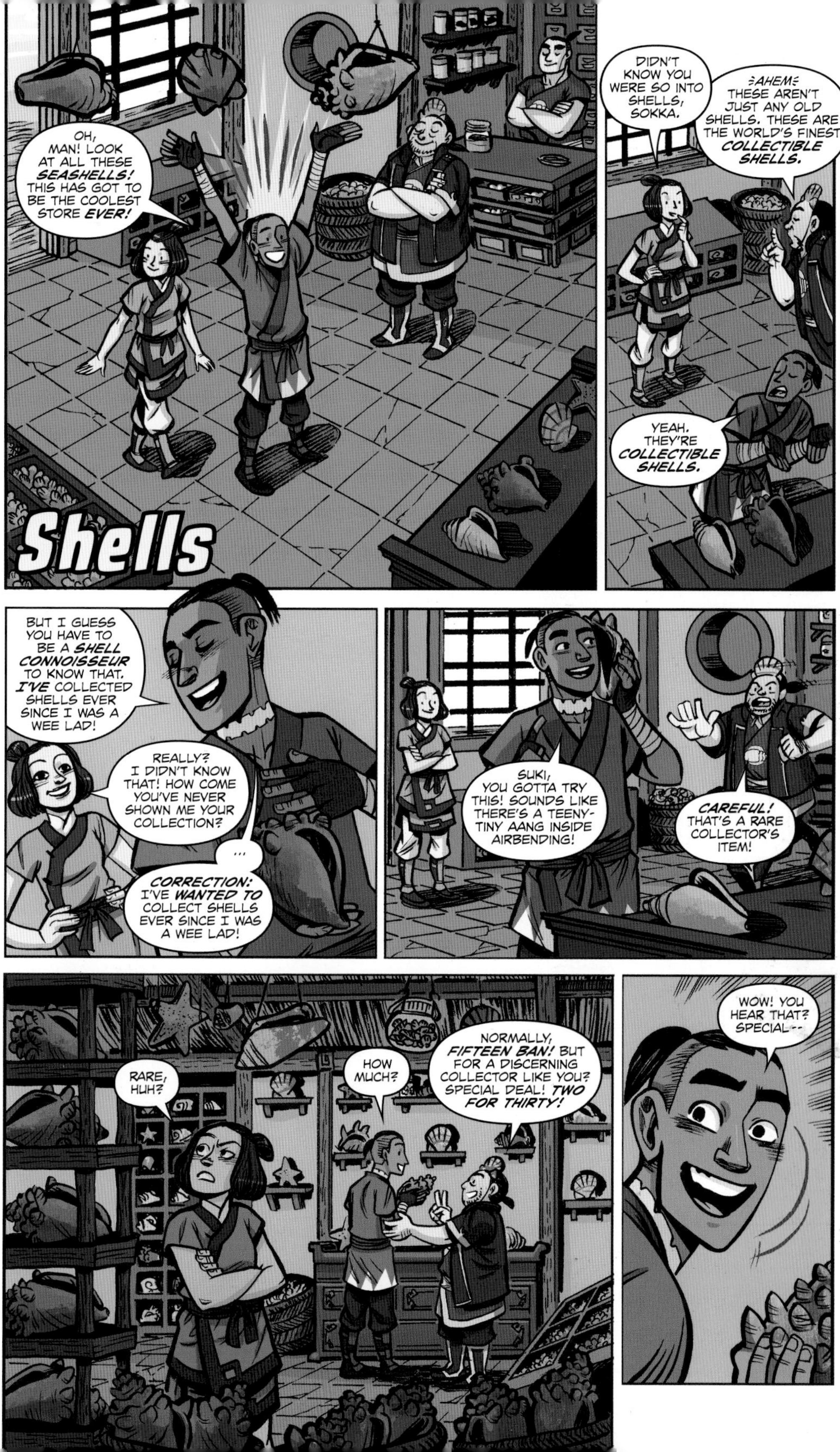
Shells
OH, MAN! LOOK AT ALL THESE SEASHELLS! THIS HAS GOT TO BE THE COOLEST STORE EVER!
DIDN'T KNOW YOU WERE SO INTO SHELLS, SOKKA.
AHEM THESE AREN'T JUST ANY OLD SHELLS. THESE ARE THE WORLD'S FINEST COLLECTIBLE SHELLS.
YEAH. THEY'RE COLLECTIBLE SHELLS.
BUT I GUESS YOU HAVE TO BE A SHELL CONNOISSEUR TO KNOW THAT. I'VE COLLECTED SHELLS EVER SINCE I WAS A WEE LAD!
REALLY? I DIDN'T KNOW THAT! HOW COME YOU'VE NEVER SHOWN ME YOUR COLLECTION?
...
CORRECTION: I'VE WANTED TO COLLECT SHELLS EVER SINCE I WAS A WEE LAD!
SUKI, YOU GOTTA TRY THIS! SOUNDS LIKE THERE'S A TEENY-TINY AANG INSIDE AIRBENDING!
CAREFUL! THAT'S A RARE COLLECTOR'S ITEM!
RARE, HUH?
HOW MUCH?
NORMALLY, FIFTEEN BAN! BUT FOR A DISCERNING COLLECTOR LIKE YOU? SPECIAL DEAL! TWO FOR THIRTY!
WOW! YOU HEAR THAT? SPECIAL--

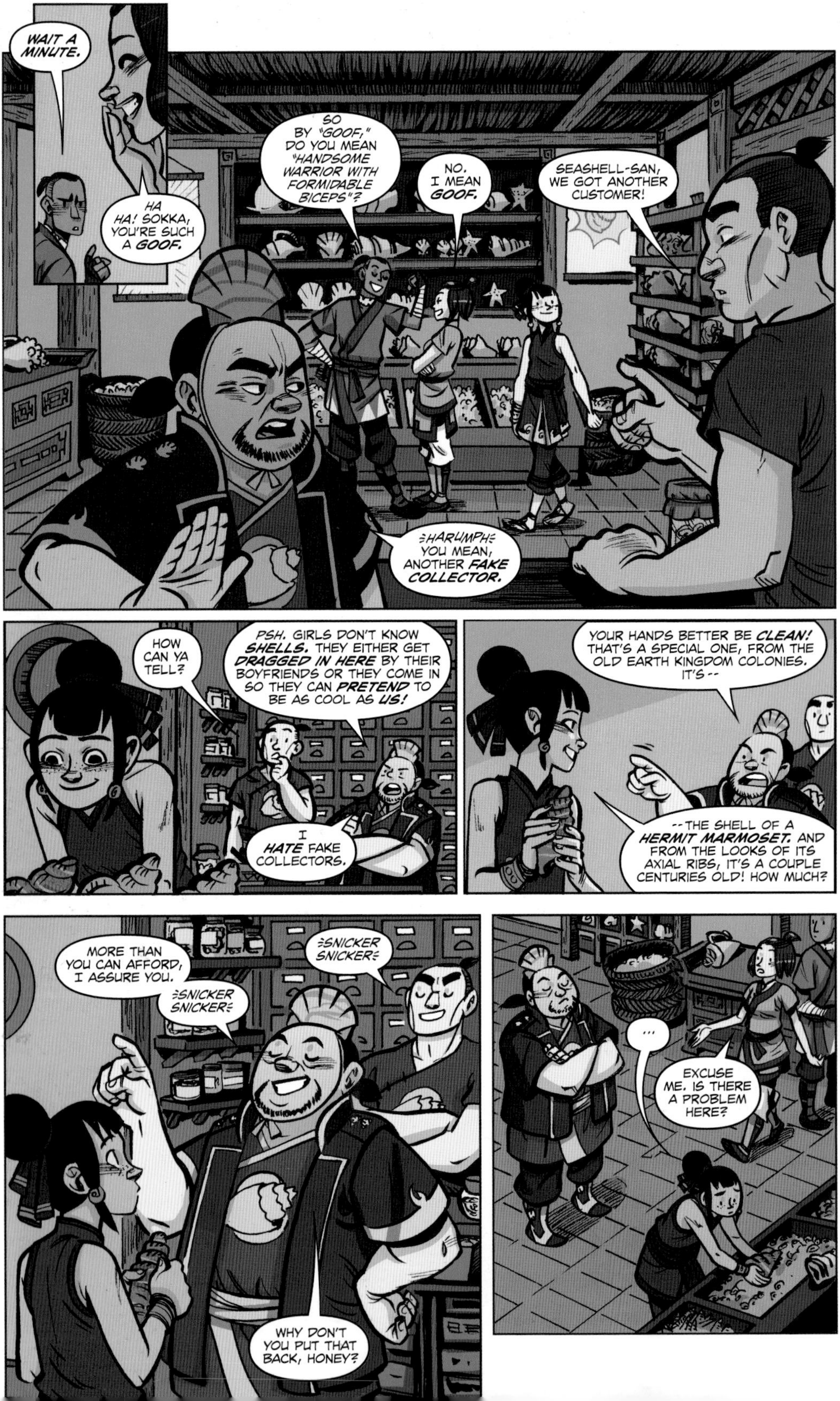
WAIT A MINUTE.
HA HA! SOKKA, YOU'RE SUCH A GOOF.
SO BY "GOOF," DO YOU MEAN "HANDSOME WARRIOR WITH FORMIDABLE BICEPS"?
NO. I MEAN GOOF.
SEASHELL-SAN, WE GOT ANOTHER CUSTOMER!
HARUMPH YOU MEAN, ANOTHER FAKE COLLECTOR.
HOW CAN YA TELL?
PSH. GIRLS DON'T KNOW SHELLS. THEY EITHER GET DRAGGED IN HERE BY THEIR BOYFRIENDS OR THEY COME IN SO THEY CAN PRETEND TO BE AS COOL AS US!
I HATE FAKE COLLECTORS.
YOUR HANDS BETTER BE CLEAN! THAT'S A SPECIAL ONE, FROM THE OLD EARTH KINGDOM COLONIES. IT'S --
--THE SHELL OF A HERMIT MARMOSET. AND FROM THE LOOKS OF ITS AXIAL RIBS, IT'S A COUPLE CENTURIES OLD! HOW MUCH?
MORE THAN YOU CAN AFFORD, I ASSURE YOU.
SNICKER SNICKER
SNICKER SNICKER
WHY DON'T YOU PUT THAT BACK, HONEY?
...
EXCUSE ME. IS THERE A PROBLEM HERE?

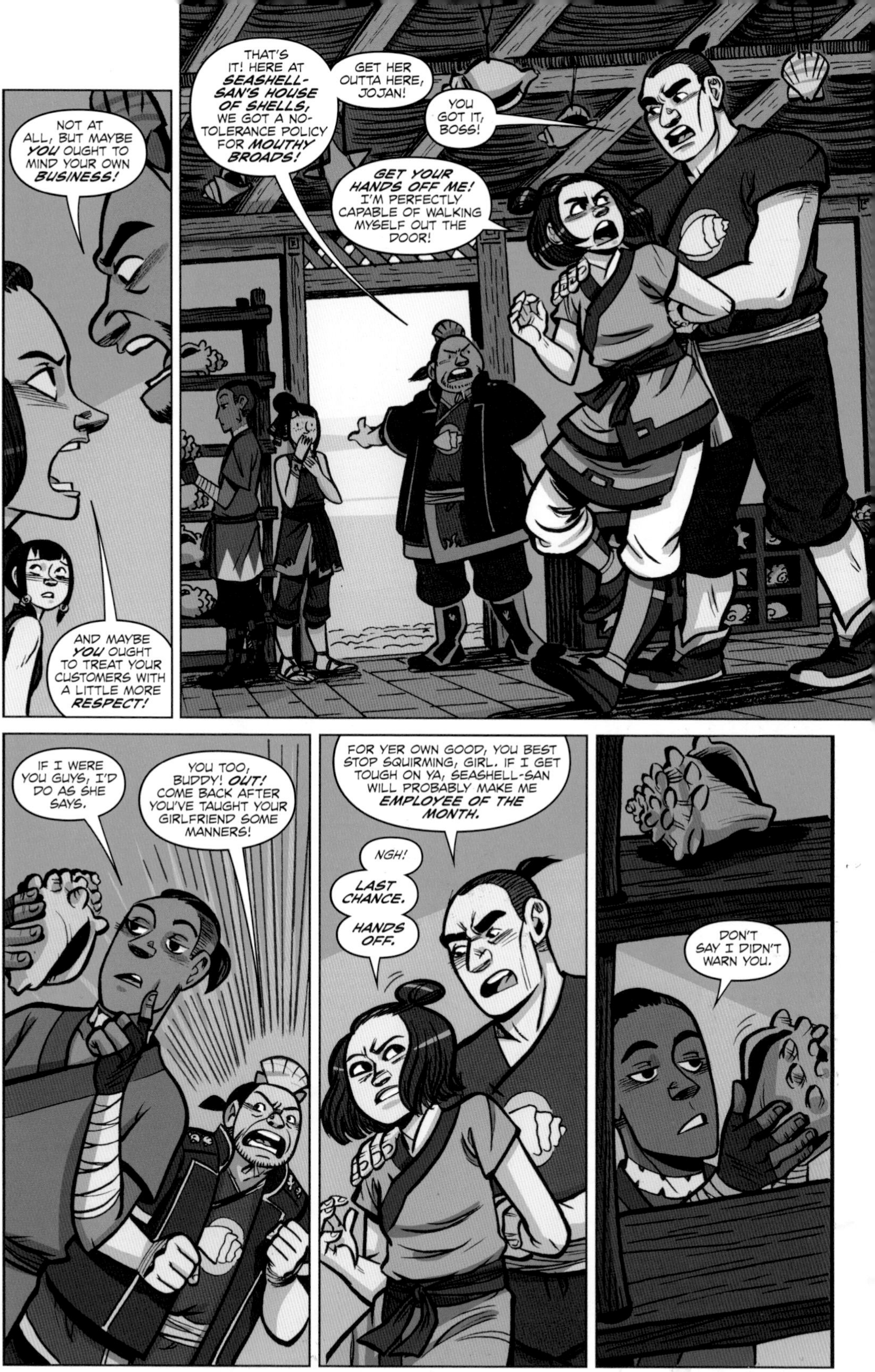
NOT AT ALL, BUT MAYBE YOU OUGHT TO MIND YOUR OWN BUSINESS!
AND MAYBE YOU OUGHT TO TREAT YOUR CUSTOMERS WITH A LITTLE MORE RESPECT!
THAT'S IT! HERE AT SEASHELL-SAN'S HOUSE OF SHELLS, WE GOT A NO-TOLERANCE POLICY FOR MOUTHY BROADS!
GET HER OUTTA HERE, JOJAN!
YOU GOT IT, BOSS!
GET YOUR HANDS OFF ME! I'M PERFECTLY CAPABLE OF WALKING MYSELF OUT THE DOOR!
IF I WERE YOU GUYS, I'D DO AS SHE SAYS.
YOU TOO, BUDDY! OUT! COME BACK AFTER YOU'VE TAUGHT YOUR GIRLFRIEND SOME MANNERS!
FOR YER OWN GOOD, YOU BEST STOP SQUIRMING, GIRL. IF I GET TOUGH ON YA, SEASHELL-SAN WILL PROBABLY MAKE ME EMPLOYEE OF THE MONTH.
NGH!
LAST CHANCE.
HANDS OFF.
DON'T SAY I DIDN'T WARN YOU.

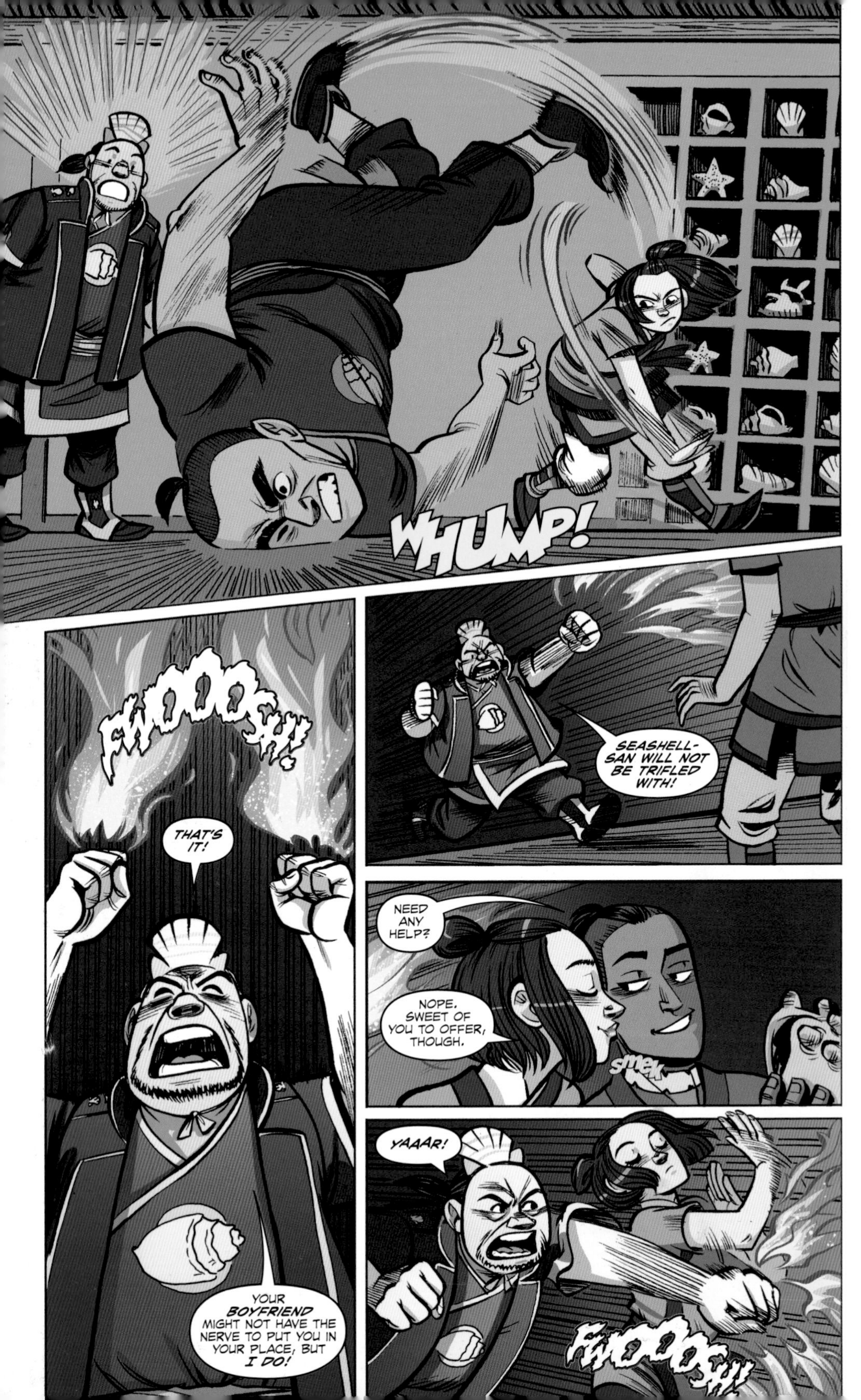
WHUMP!
FWOOOSH!
THAT'S IT!
YOUR BOYFRIEND MIGHT NOT HAVE THE NERVE TO PUT YOU IN YOUR PLACE, BUT I DO!
SEASHELL-SAN WILL NOT BE TRIFLED WITH!
NEED ANY HELP?
NOPE. SWEET OF YOU TO OFFER, THOUGH.
SMEK
YAAAR!
FWOOOSH!

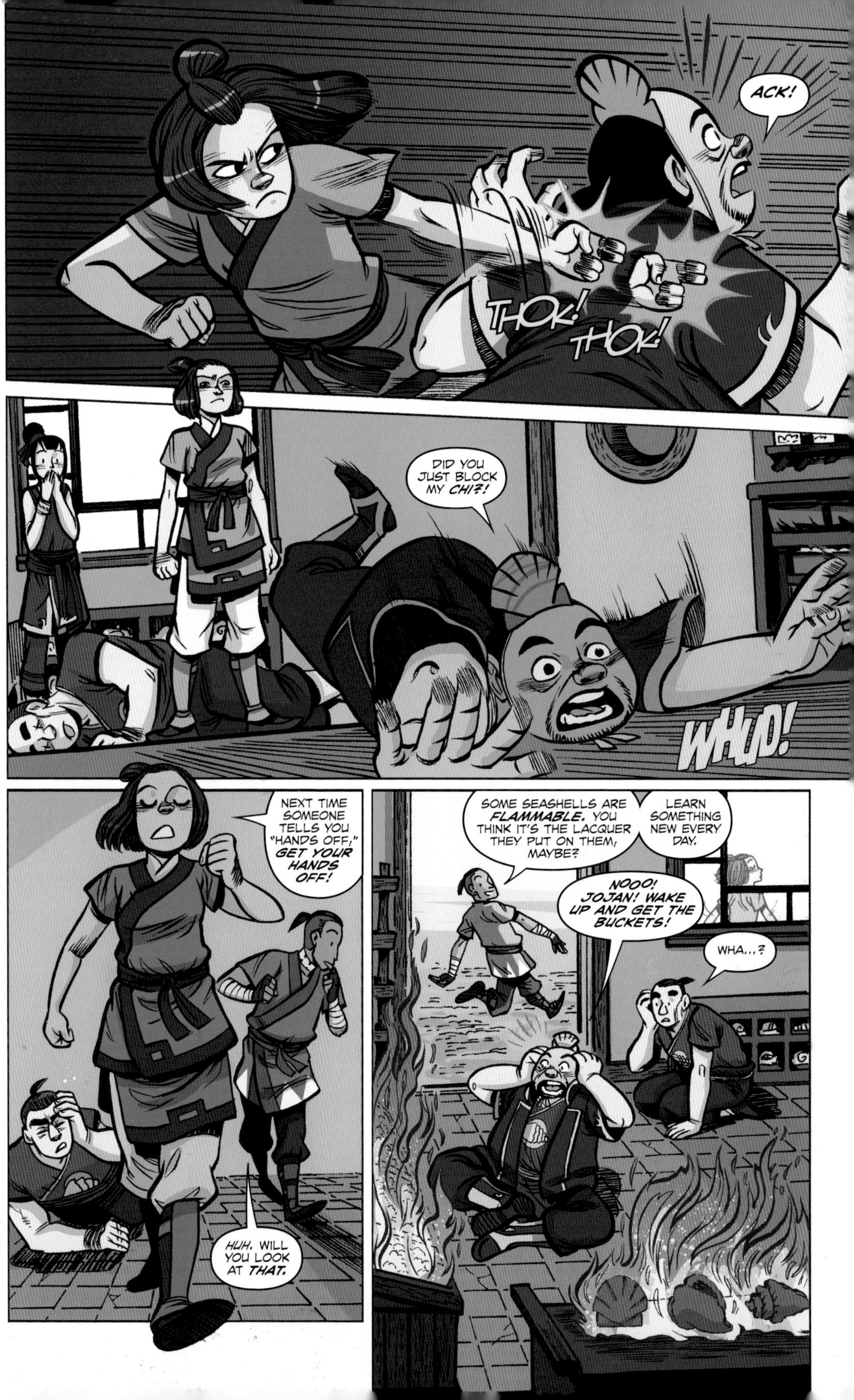
ACK!
THOK! THOK!
DID YOU JUST BLOCK MY CHI?!
WHUD!
NEXT TIME SOMEONE TELLS YOU "HANDS OFF," GET YOUR HANDS OFF!
HUH. WILL YOU LOOK AT THAT.
SOME SEASHELLS ARE FLAMMABLE. YOU THINK IT'S THE LACQUER THEY PUT ON THEM, MAYBE?
LEARN SOMETHING NEW EVERY DAY.
NOOO! JOJAN! WAKE UP AND GET THE BUCKETS!
WHA...?

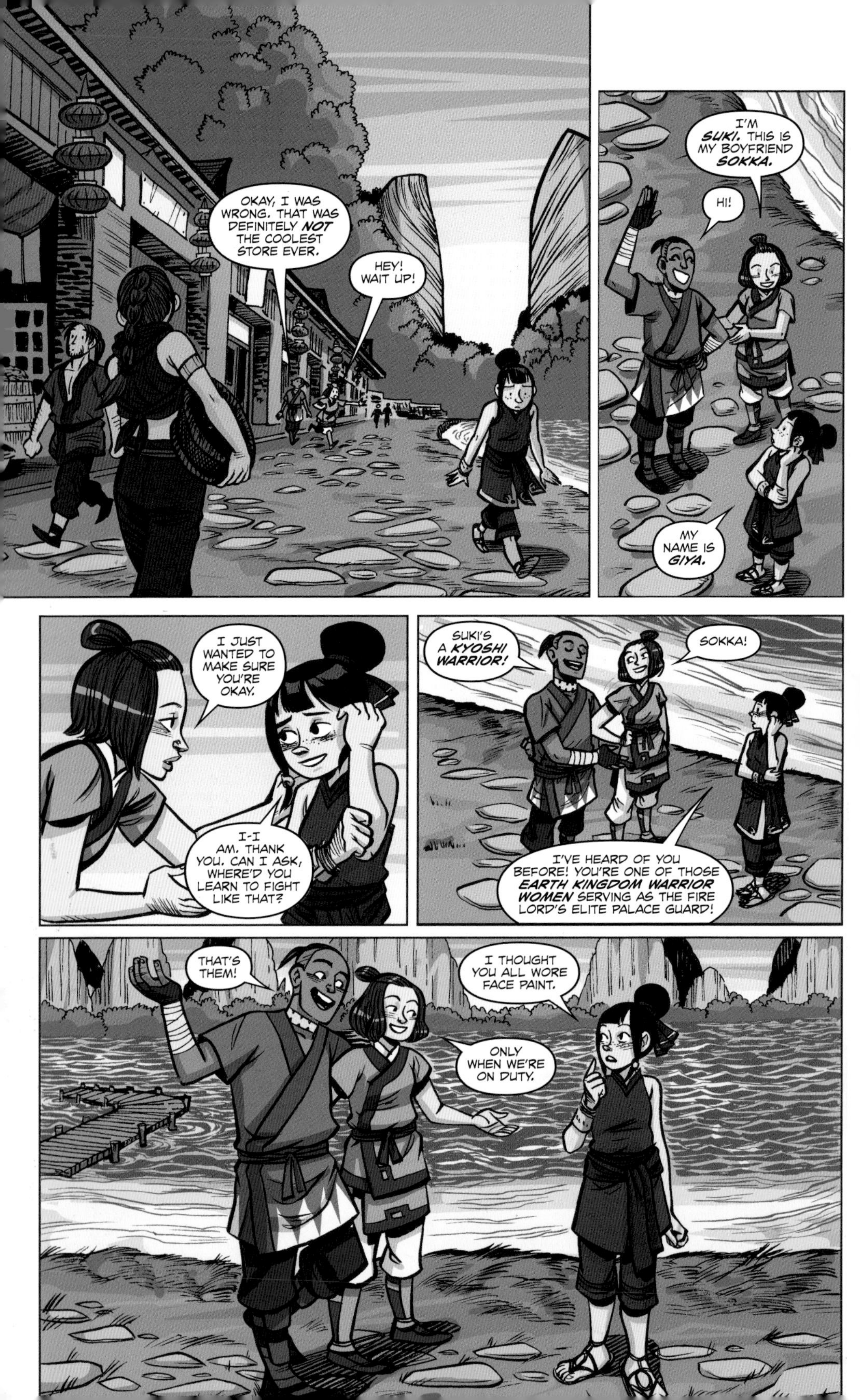

OKAY, I WAS WRONG. THAT WAS DEFINITELY NOT THE COOLEST STORE EVER.
HEY! WAIT UP!
I'M SUKI. THIS IS MY BOYFRIEND SOKKA.
HI!
MY NAME IS GIYA.
I JUST WANTED TO MAKE SURE YOU'RE OKAY.
I-I AM. THANK YOU. CAN I ASK, WHERE'D YOU LEARN TO FIGHT LIKE THAT?
SUKI'S A KYOSHI WARRIOR!
SOKKA!
I'VE HEARD OF YOU BEFORE! YOU'RE ONE OF THOSE EARTH KINGDOM WARRIOR WOMEN SERVING AS THE FIRE LORD'S ELITE PALACE GUARD!
THAT'S THEM!
I THOUGHT YOU ALL WORE FACE PAINT.
ONLY WHEN WE'RE ON DUTY.

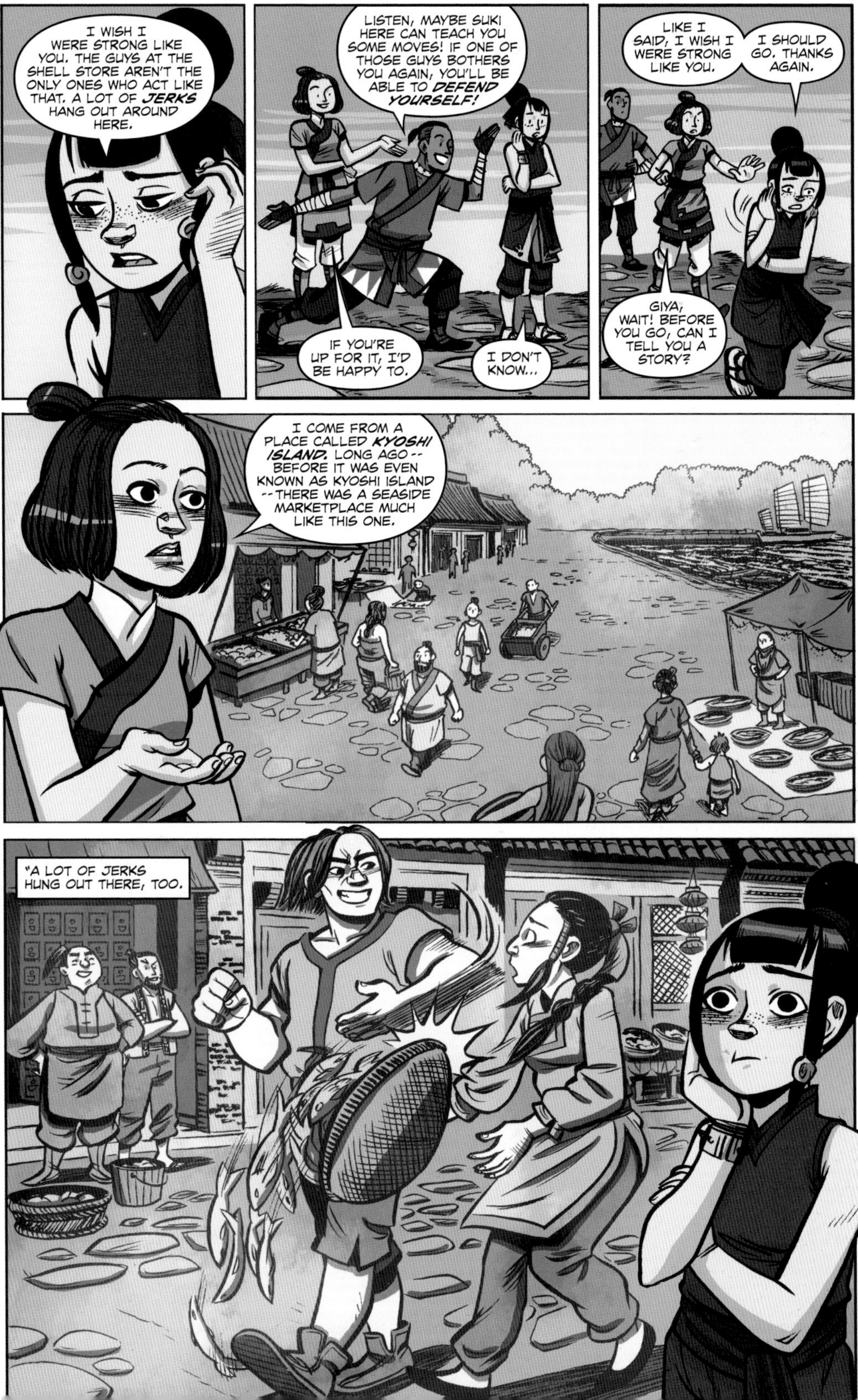
I WISH I WERE STRONG LIKE YOU. THE GUYS AT THE SHELL STORE AREN'T THE ONLY ONES WHO ACT LIKE THAT. A LOT OF JERKS HANG OUT AROUND HERE.
LISTEN, MAYBE SUKI HERE CAN TEACH YOU SOME MOVES! IF ONE OF THOSE GUYS BOTHERS YOU AGAIN, YOU'LL BE ABLE TO DEFEND YOURSELF!
IF YOU'RE UP FOR IT, I'D BE HAPPY TO.
I DON'T KNOW...
LIKE I SAID, I WISH I WERE STRONG LIKE YOU.
I SHOULD GO. THANKS AGAIN.
GIYA, WAIT! BEFORE YOU GO, CAN I TELL YOU A STORY?
I COME FROM A PLACE CALLED KYOSHI ISLAND. LONG AGO -- BEFORE IT WAS EVEN KNOWN AS KYOSHI ISLAND -- THERE WAS A SEASIDE MARKETPLACE MUCH LIKE THIS ONE.
"A LOT OF JERKS HUNG OUT THERE, TOO.

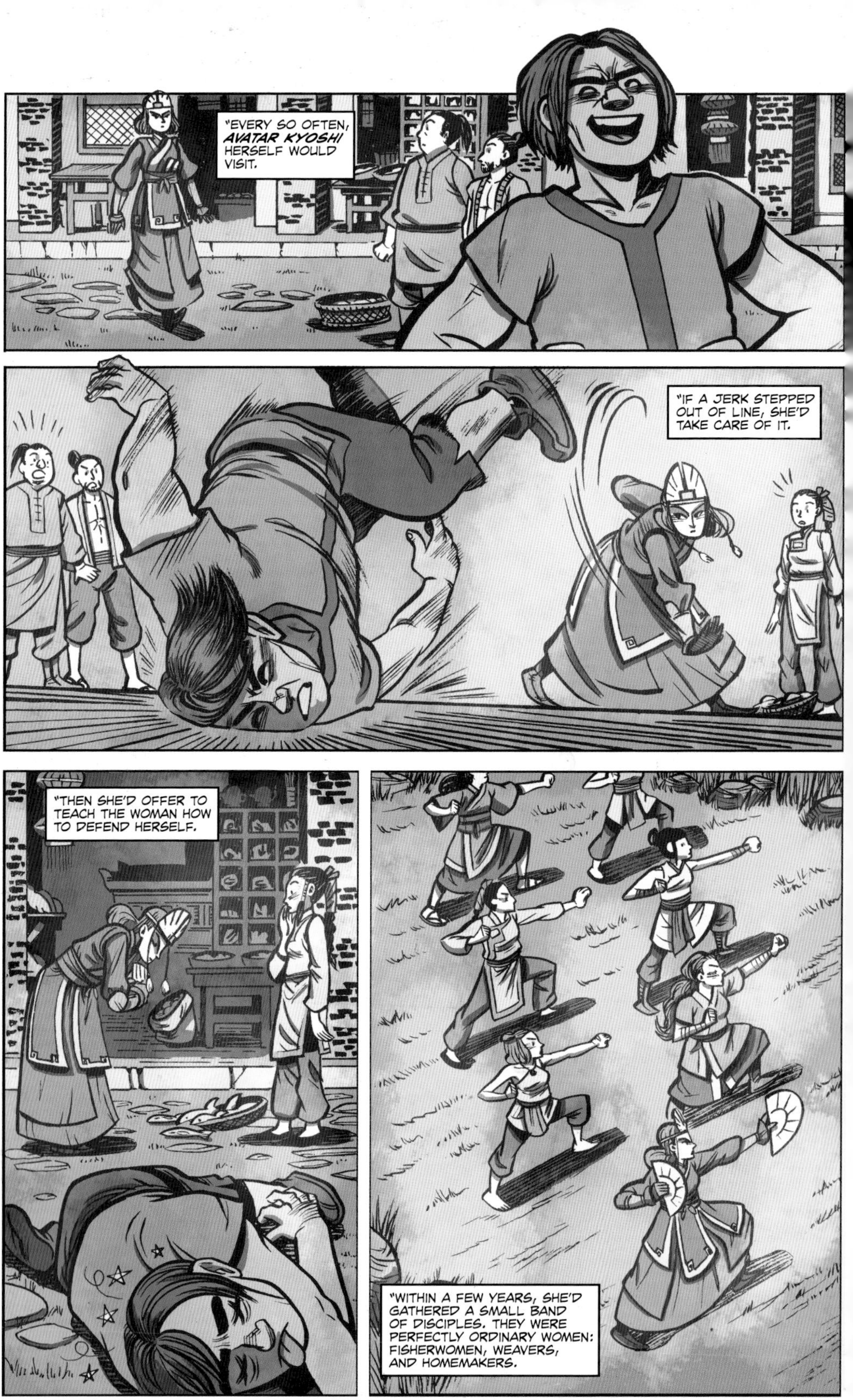
"EVERY SO OFTEN, AVATAR KYOSHI HERSELF WOULD VISIT.
"IF A JERK STEPPED OUT OF LINE, SHE'D TAKE CARE OF IT.
"THEN SHE'D OFFER TO TEACH THE WOMAN HOW TO DEFEND HERSELF.
"WITHIN A FEW YEARS, SHE'D GATHERED A SMALL BAND OF DISCIPLES. THEY WERE PERFECTLY ORDINARY WOMEN: FISHERWOMEN, WEAVERS, AND HOMEMAKERS.

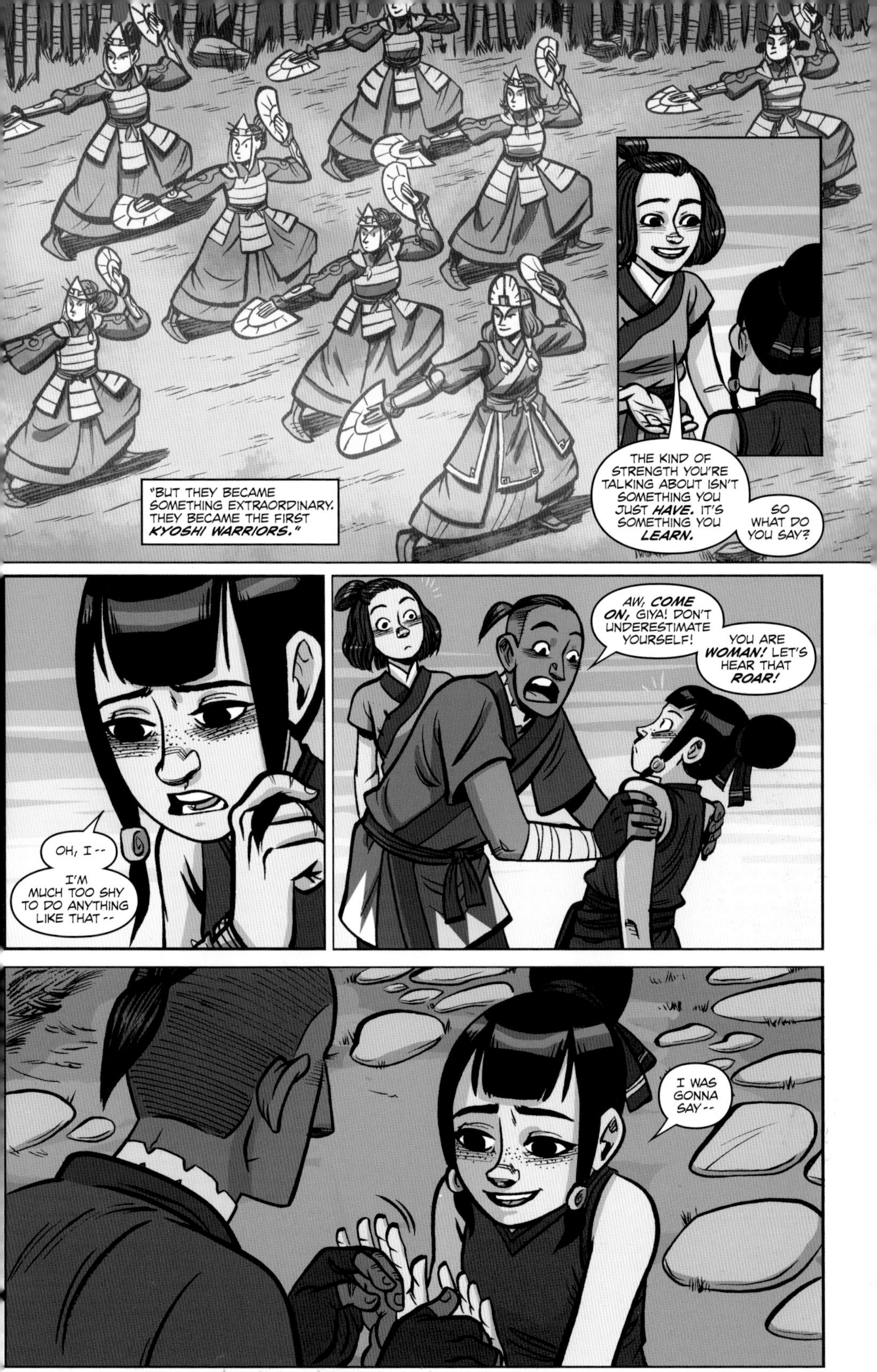
"BUT THEY BECAME SOMETHING EXTRAORDINARY. THEY BECAME THE FIRST *KYOSHI WARRIORS.*"
THE KIND OF STRENGTH YOU'RE TALKING ABOUT ISN'T SOMETHING YOU JUST *HAVE.* IT'S SOMETHING YOU *LEARN.*
SO WHAT DO YOU SAY?
OH, I --
I'M MUCH TOO SHY TO DO ANYTHING LIKE THAT --
AW, *COME ON,* GIYA! DON'T UNDERESTIMATE YOURSELF!
YOU ARE *WOMAN!* LET'S HEAR THAT *ROAR!*
I WAS GONNA SAY --

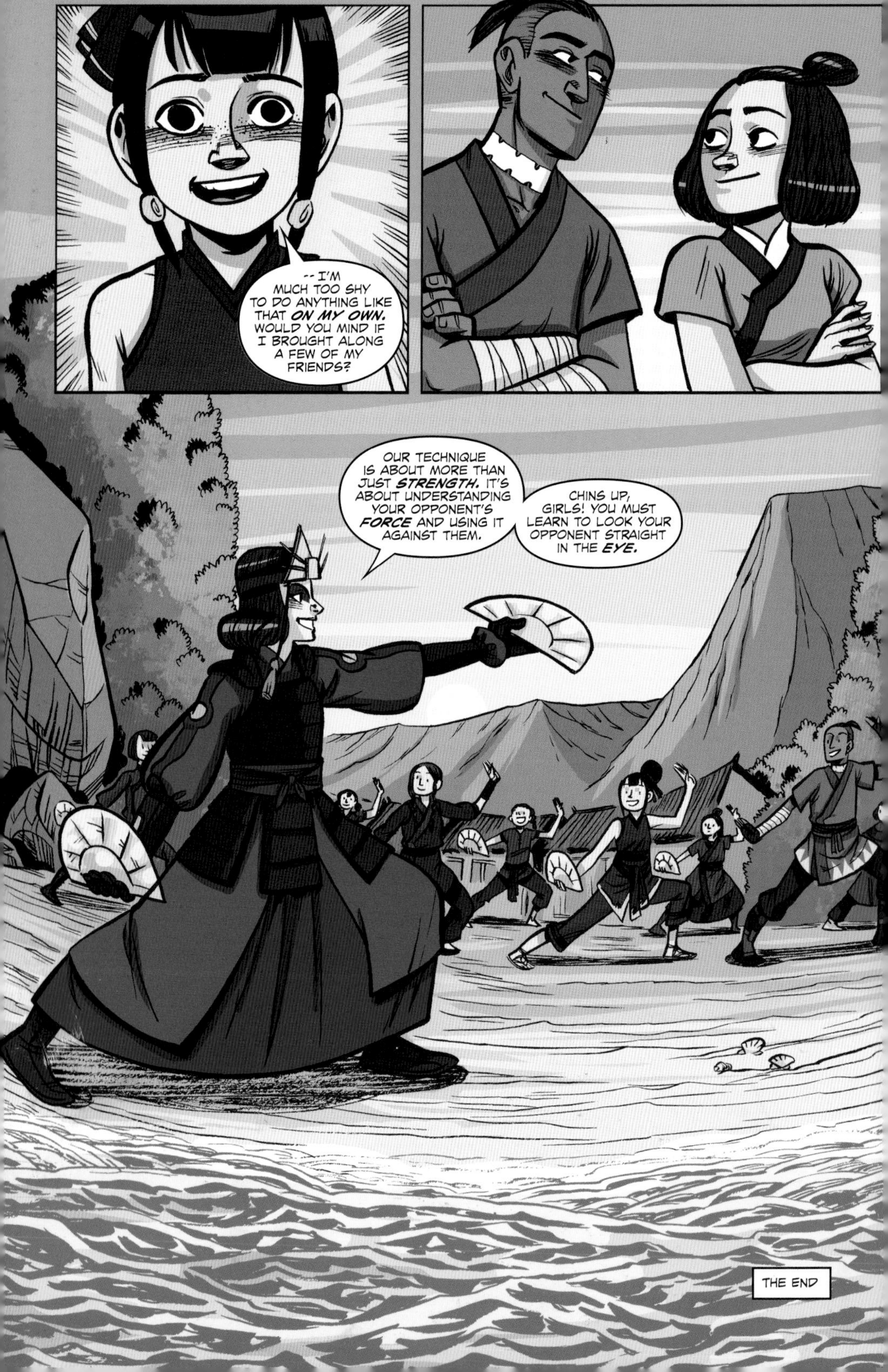
-- I'M MUCH TOO SHY TO DO ANYTHING LIKE THAT ON MY OWN. WOULD YOU MIND IF I BROUGHT ALONG A FEW OF MY FRIENDS?
OUR TECHNIQUE IS ABOUT MORE THAN JUST STRENGTH. IT'S ABOUT UNDERSTANDING YOUR OPPONENT'S FORCE AND USING IT AGAINST THEM.
CHINS UP, GIRLS! YOU MUST LEARN TO LOOK YOUR OPPONENT STRAIGHT IN THE EYE.
THE END

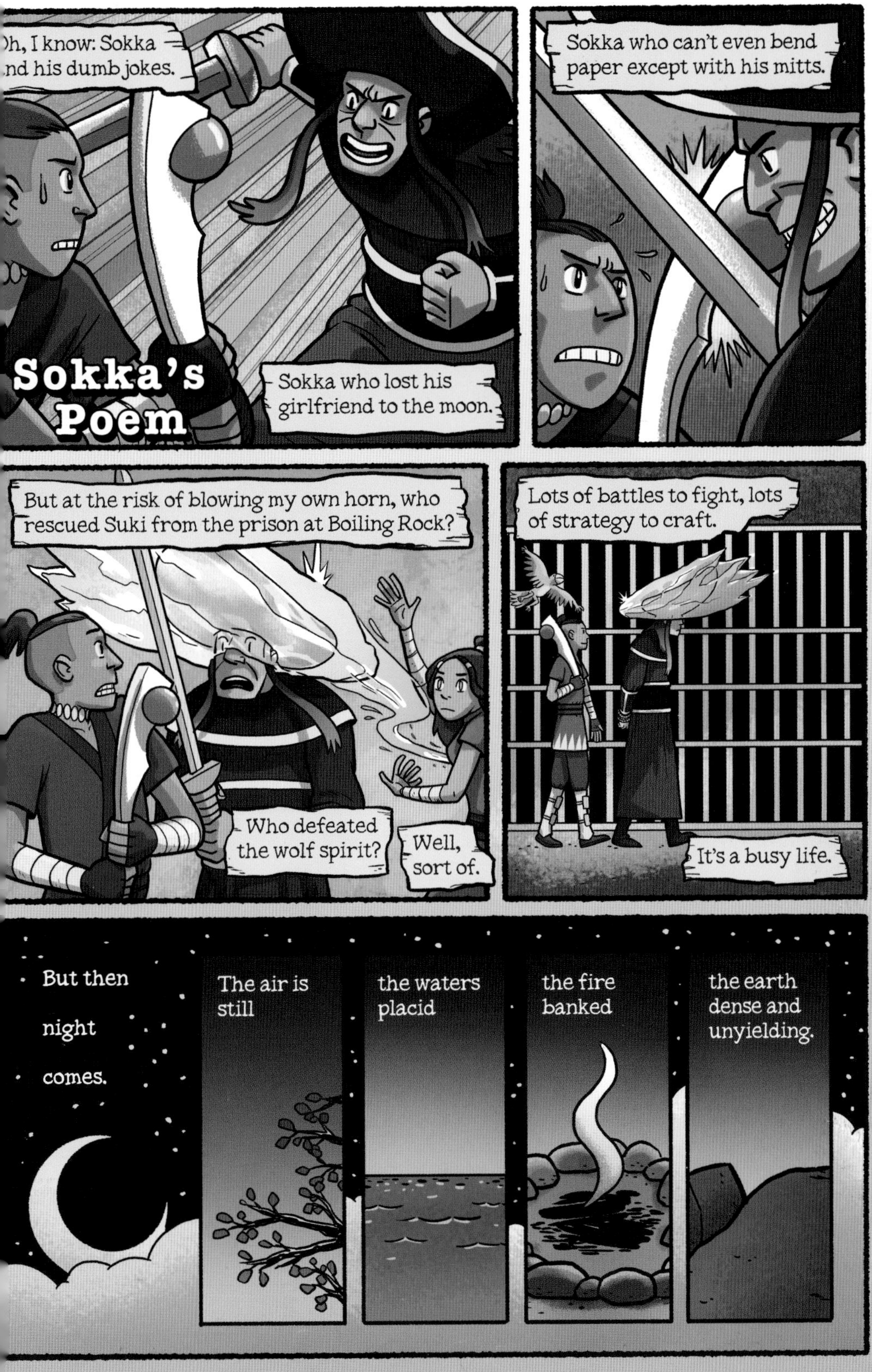

Oh, I know: Sokka and his dumb jokes.
Sokka's Poem
Sokka who lost his girlfriend to the moon.
Sokka who can't even bend paper except with his mitts.
But at the risk of blowing my own horn, who rescued Suki from the prison at Boiling Rock?
Who defeated the wolf spirit?
Well, sort of.
Lots of battles to fight, lots of strategy to craft.
It's a busy life.
But then
night
comes.
The air is still
the waters placid
the fire banked
the earth dense and unyielding.

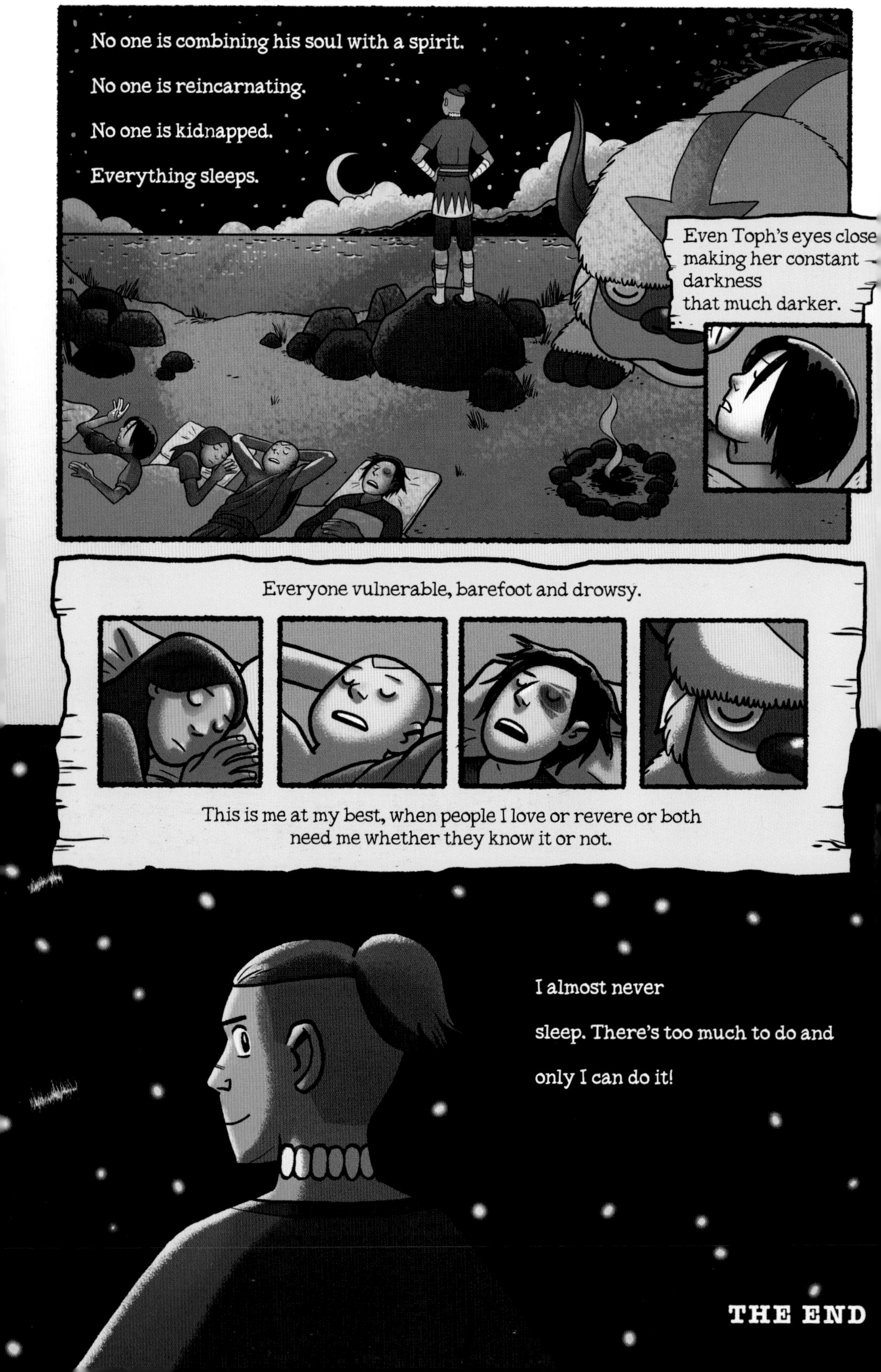
No one is combining his soul with a spirit.
No one is reincarnating.
No one is kidnapped.
Everything sleeps.
Even Toph's eyes close making her constant darkness that much darker.
Everyone vulnerable, barefoot and drowsy.
This is me at my best, when people I love or revere or both need me whether they know it or not.
I almost never
sleep. There's too much to do and
only I can do it!
THE END

TOPH AND THE BOULDER

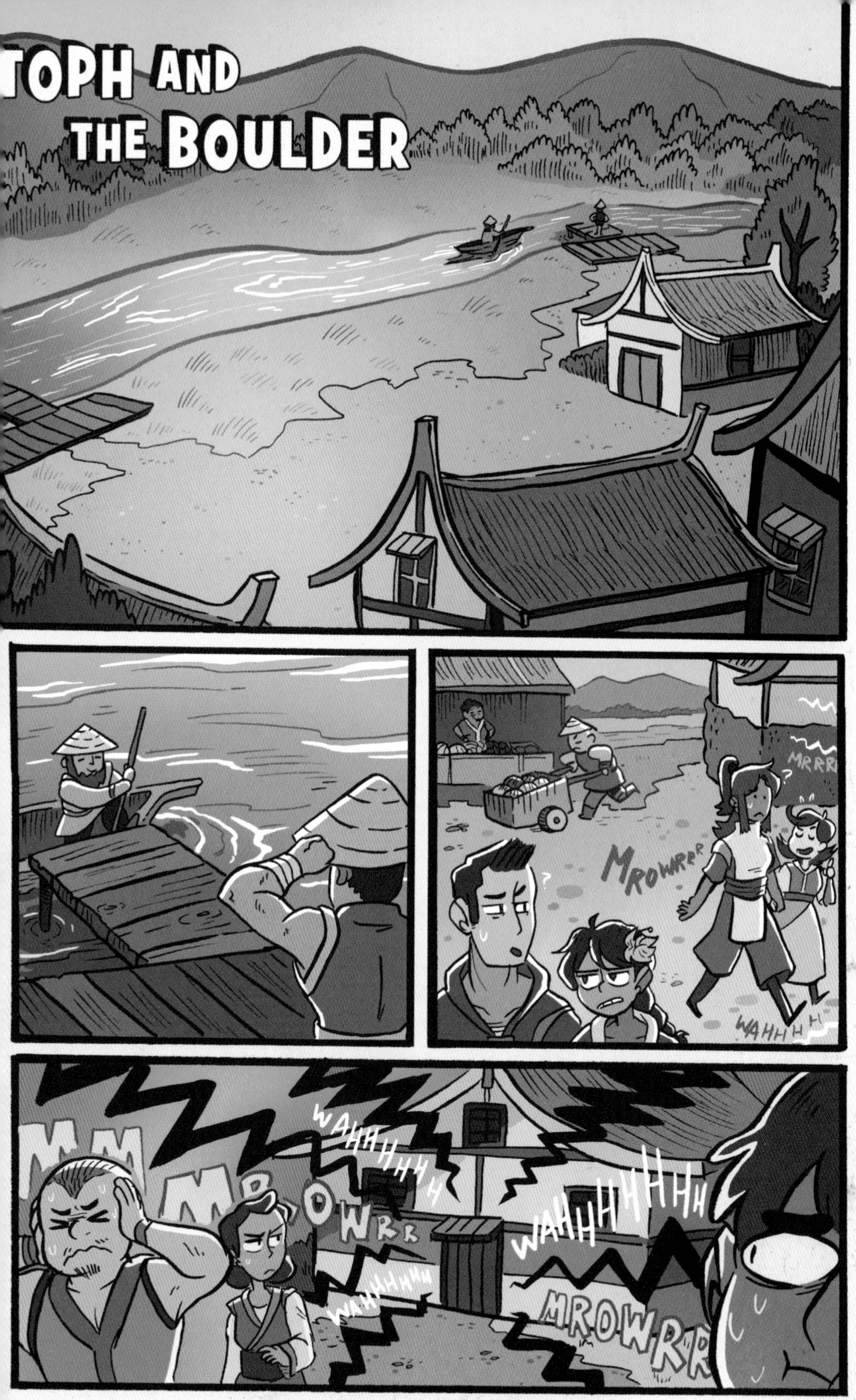

MRRR
MROWRRR
WAHHHH
MMMMBROWRR
WAHHHHHHH
WAHHHHHHHH
WAHHHHHHHHHH
MROWRR

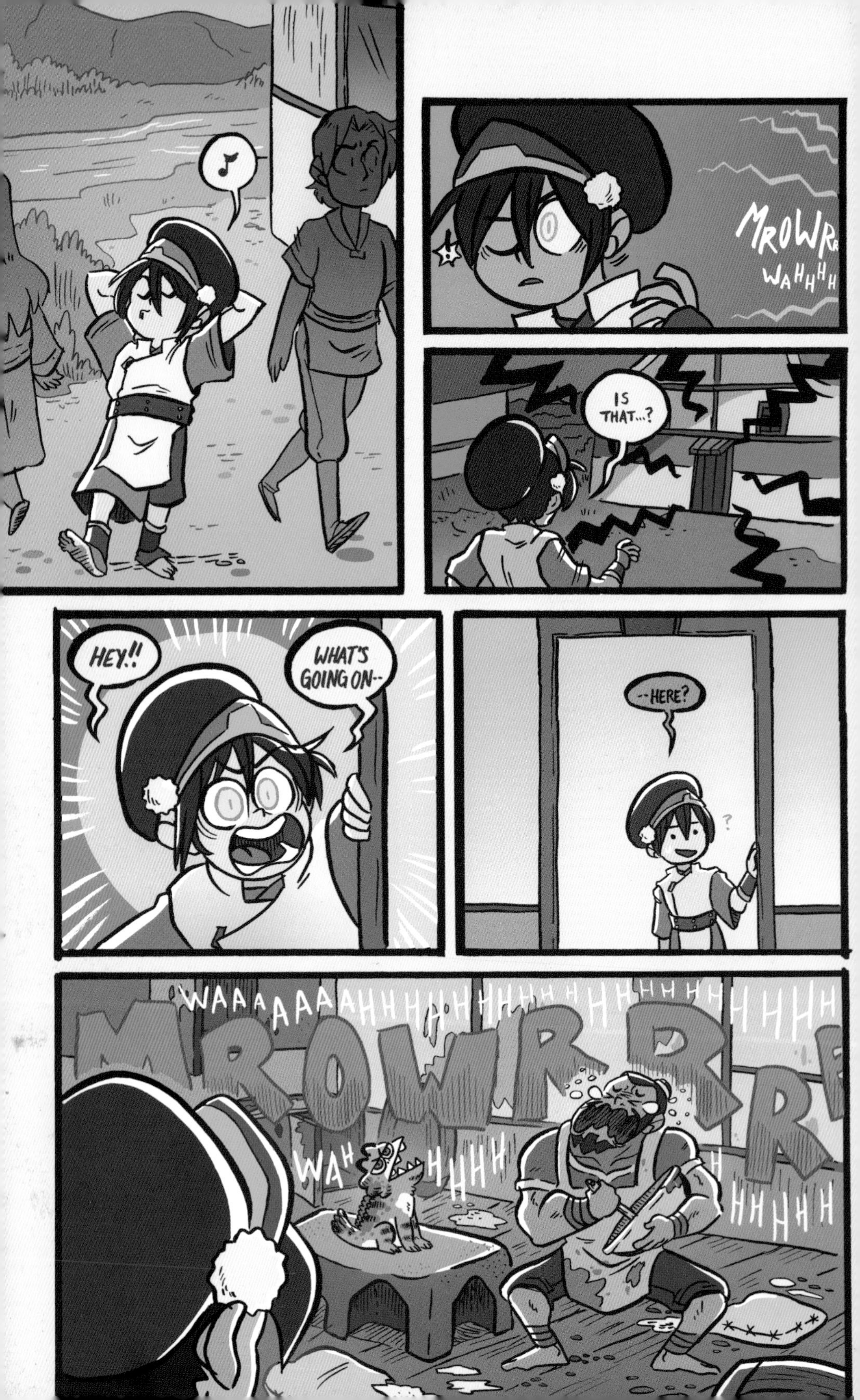
♪
MROWRR
WAHHHH
IS THAT...?
HEY!!
WHAT'S GOING ON--
--HERE?
?
WAAAAAAAHHHHHHHHHHHHHHHHHHHH
MROWRRR
WAHHHHH
HHHHH

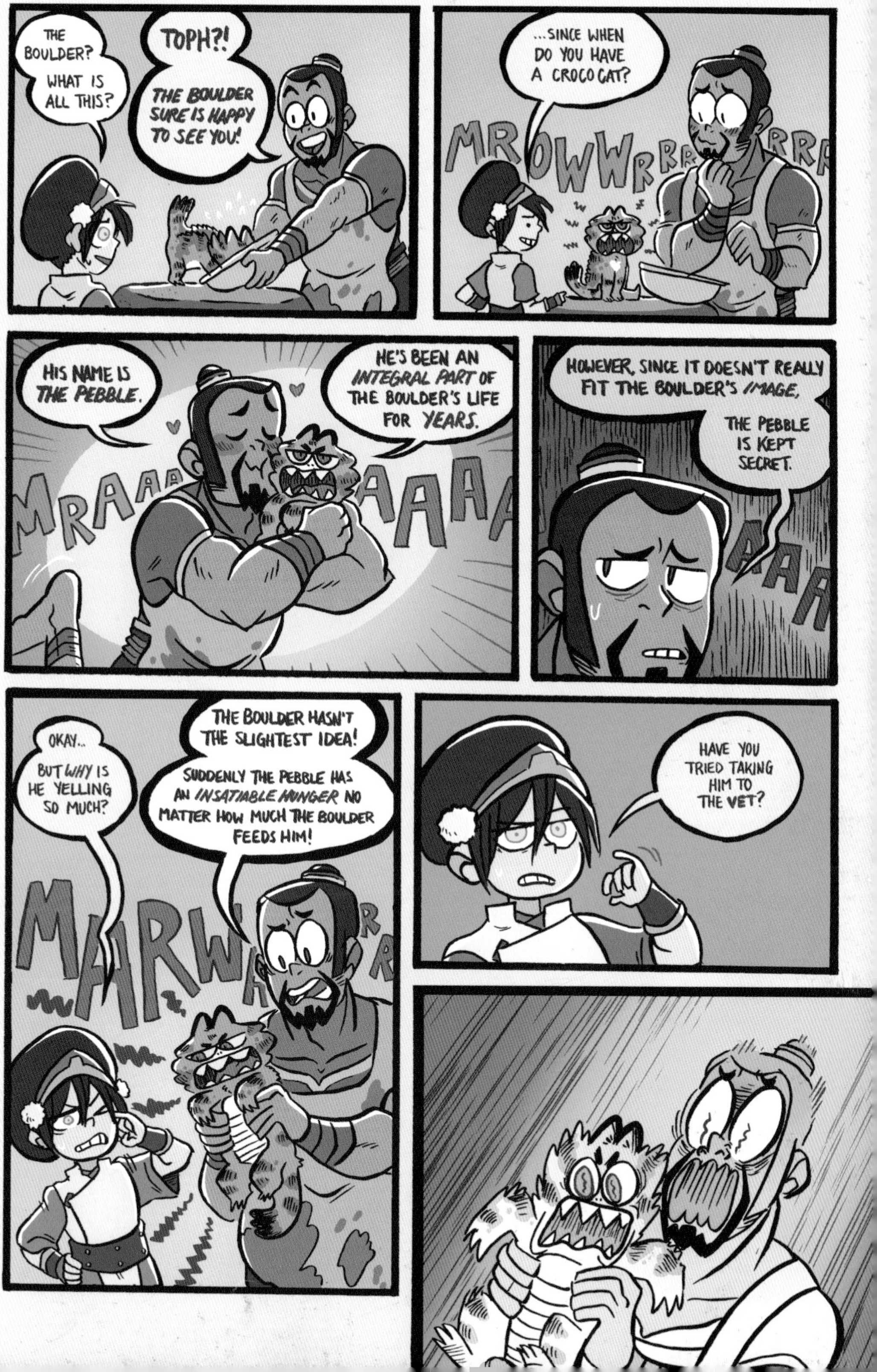
THE BOULDER? WHAT IS ALL THIS?
TOPH?! THE BOULDER SURE IS HAPPY TO SEE YOU!
...SINCE WHEN DO YOU HAVE A CROCOCAT?
MROWWRRRRRRR
HIS NAME IS THE PEBBLE.
HE'S BEEN AN INTEGRAL PART OF THE BOULDER'S LIFE FOR YEARS.
MRAAAAAAAA
HOWEVER, SINCE IT DOESN'T REALLY FIT THE BOULDER'S IMAGE,
THE PEBBLE IS KEPT SECRET.
AAA
OKAY... BUT WHY IS HE YELLING SO MUCH?
THE BOULDER HASN'T THE SLIGHTEST IDEA!
SUDDENLY THE PEBBLE HAS AN INSATIABLE HUNGER NO MATTER HOW MUCH THE BOULDER FEEDS HIM!
MARWRRR
HAVE YOU TRIED TAKING HIM TO THE VET?

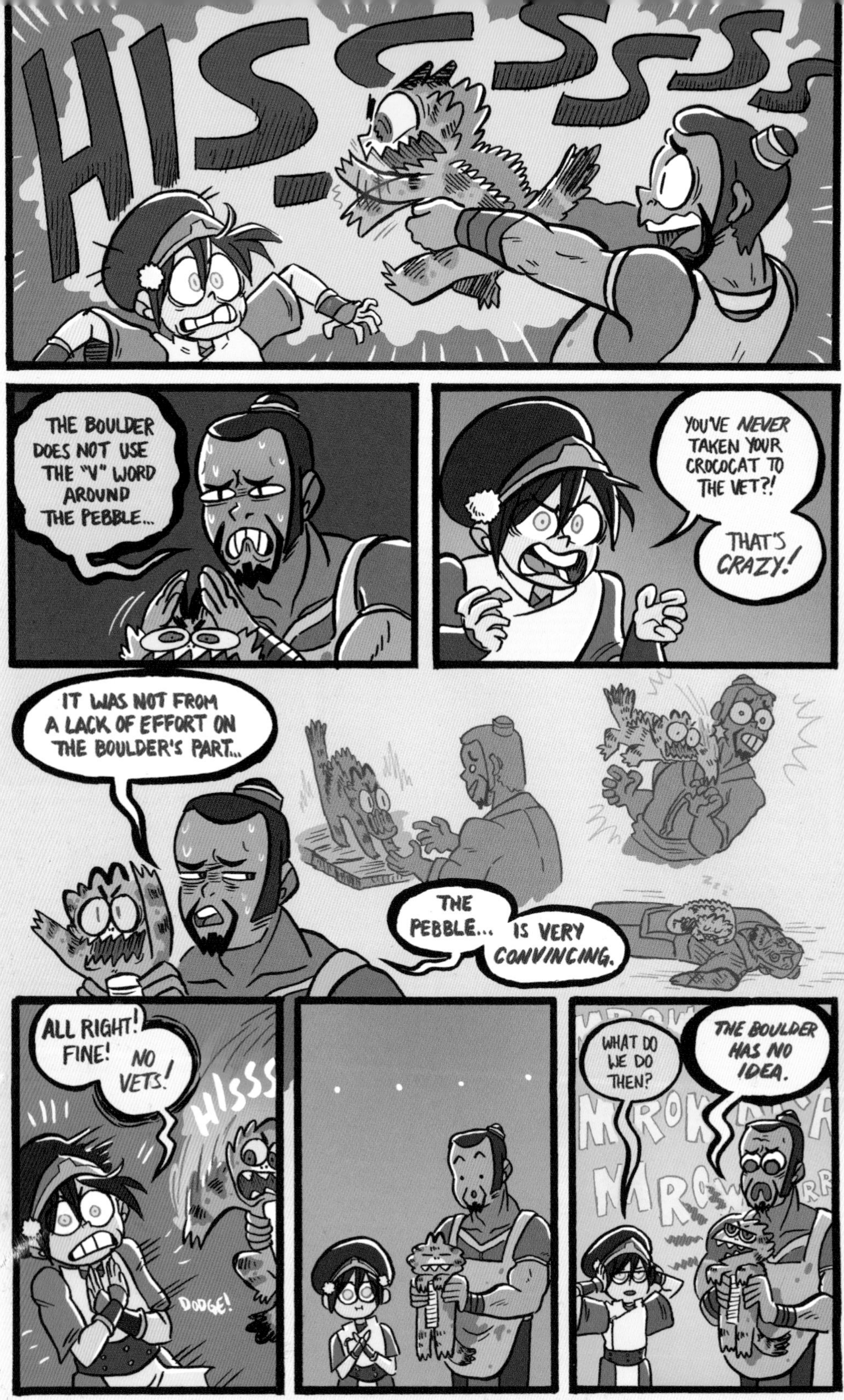
HISS-SSSS
THE BOULDER DOES NOT USE THE "V" WORD AROUND THE PEBBLE...
YOU'VE NEVER TAKEN YOUR CROCOCAT TO THE VET?!
THAT'S CRAZY!
IT WAS NOT FROM A LACK OF EFFORT ON THE BOULDER'S PART...
THE PEBBLE... IS VERY CONVINCING.
ALL RIGHT! FINE! NO VETS!
HISSS
DODGE!
WHAT DO WE DO THEN?
THE BOULDER HAS NO IDEA.

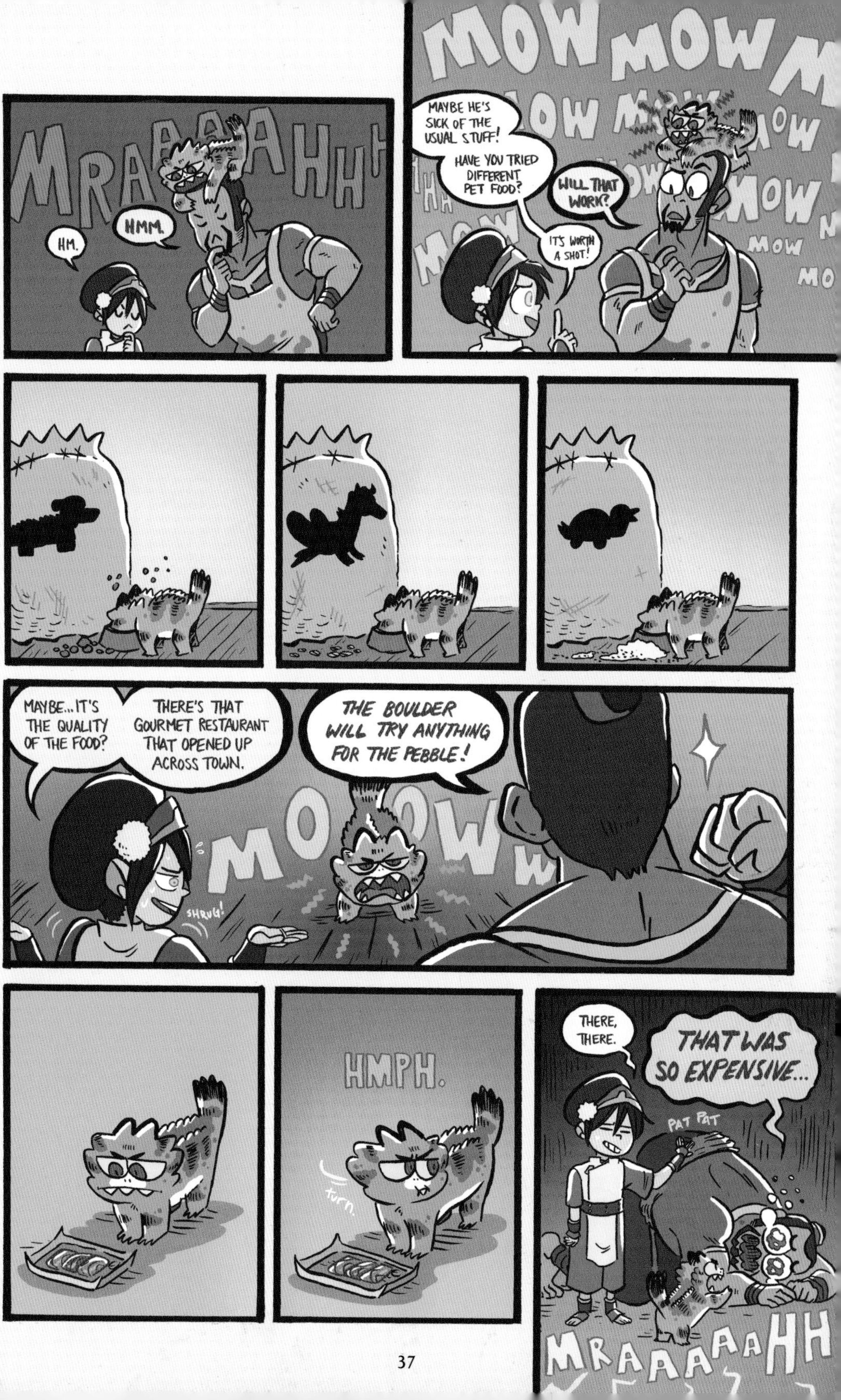
MRAAAAHHH
HM.
HMM.
MOW MOW MOW
MAYBE HE'S SICK OF THE USUAL STUFF!
HAVE YOU TRIED DIFFERENT PET FOOD?
WILL THAT WORK?
IT'S WORTH A SHOT!
MOW
MAYBE... IT'S THE QUALITY OF THE FOOD?
THERE'S THAT GOURMET RESTAURANT THAT OPENED UP ACROSS TOWN.
THE BOULDER WILL TRY ANYTHING FOR THE PEBBLE!
MOOWW
SHRUG!
HMPH.
turn.
THERE, THERE.
THAT WAS SO EXPENSIVE...
PAT PAT
MRAAAAAAHH

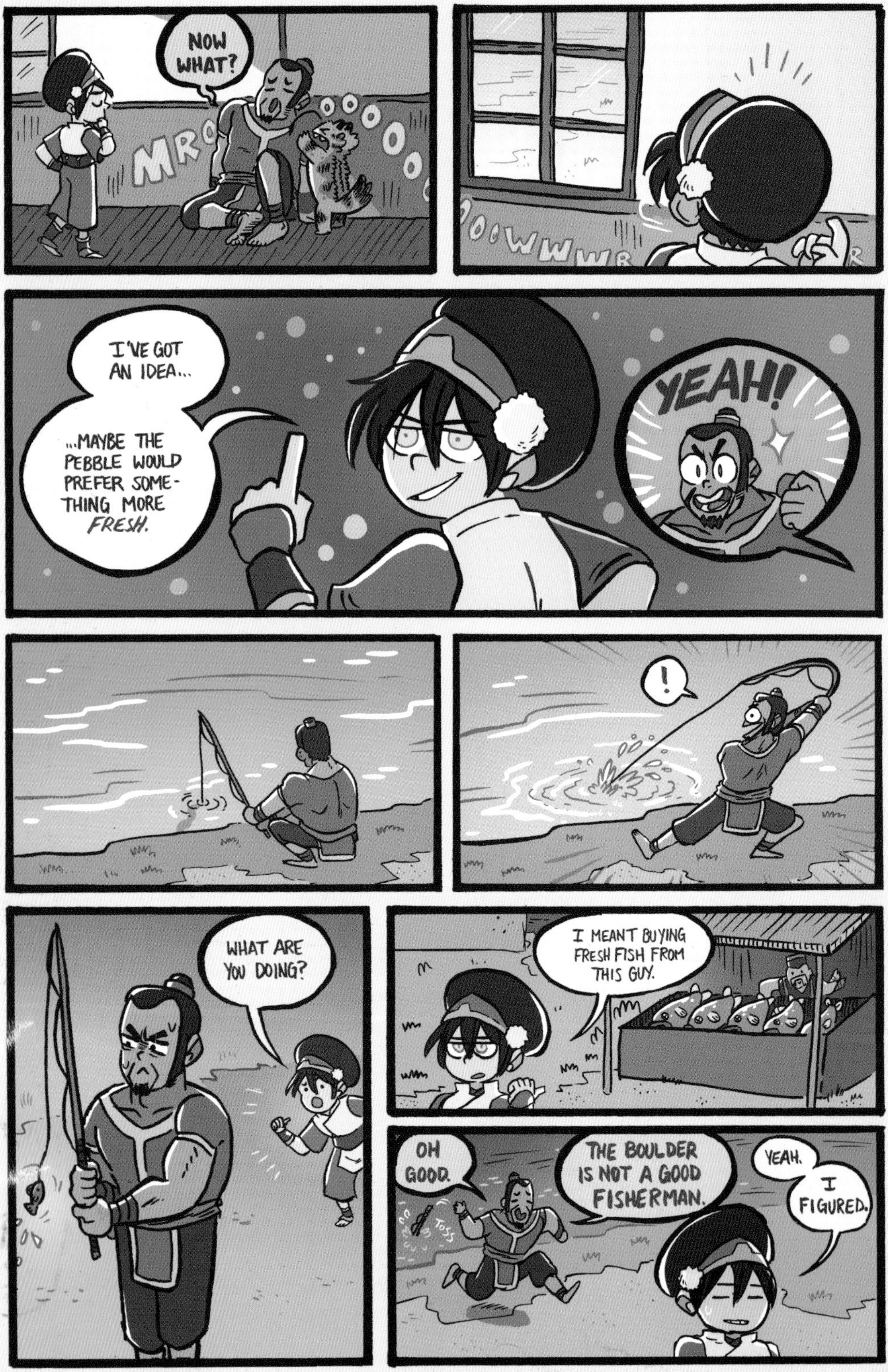
NOW WHAT?
MROOOOOOOOOWWWWR
I'VE GOT AN IDEA...
...MAYBE THE PEBBLE WOULD PREFER SOMETHING MORE FRESH.
YEAH!
!
WHAT ARE YOU DOING?
I MEANT BUYING FRESH FISH FROM THIS GUY.
OH GOOD.
THE BOULDER IS NOT A GOOD FISHERMAN.
YEAH.
I FIGURED.

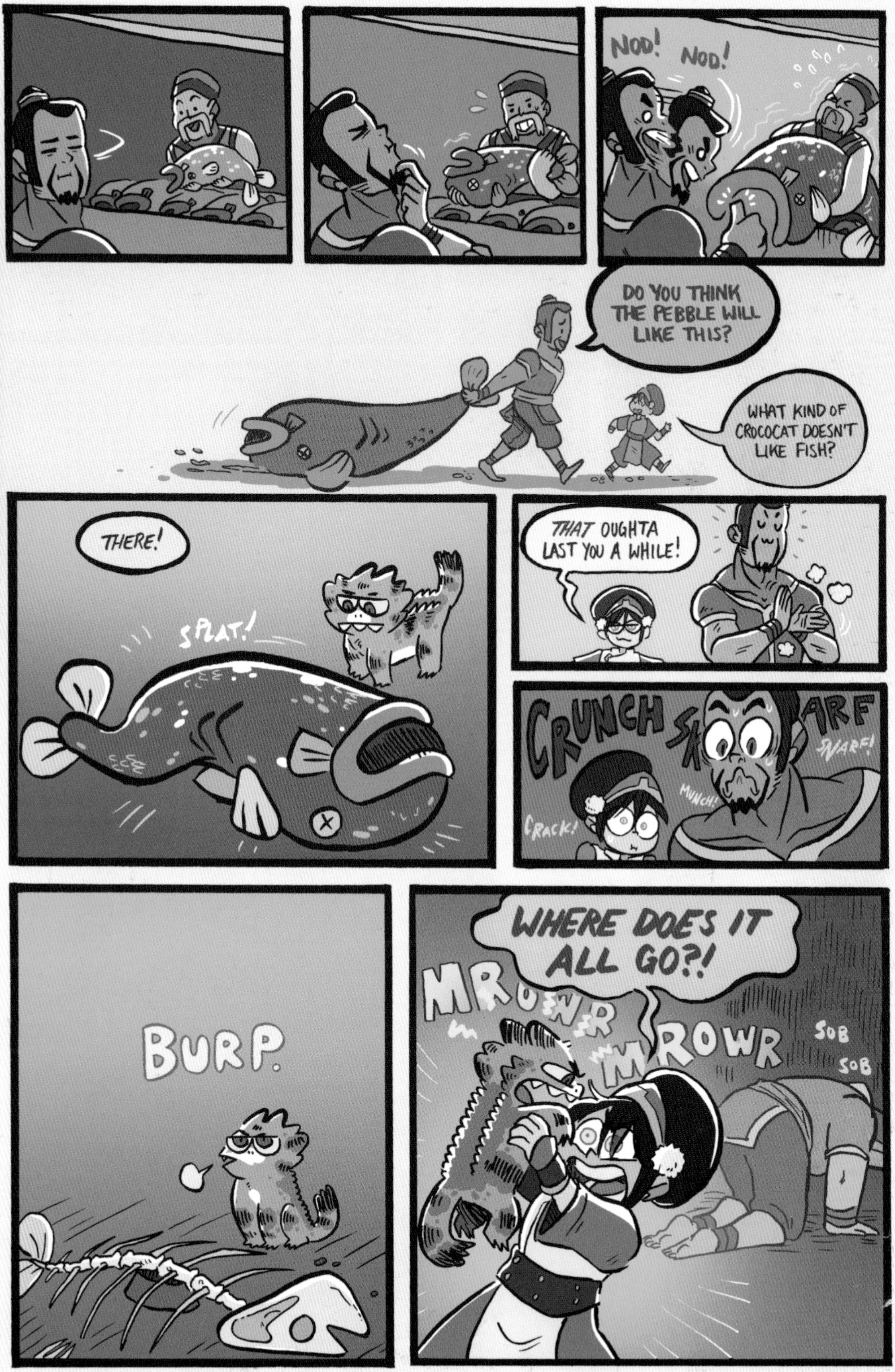
NOD! NOD!
DO YOU THINK THE PEBBLE WILL LIKE THIS?
WHAT KIND OF CROCOCAT DOESN'T LIKE FISH?
THERE!
SPLAT!
THAT OUGHTA LAST YOU A WHILE!
CRUNCH
SNARF!
MUNCH!
CRACK!
BURP.
WHERE DOES IT ALL GO?!
MROWR
SOB
SOB

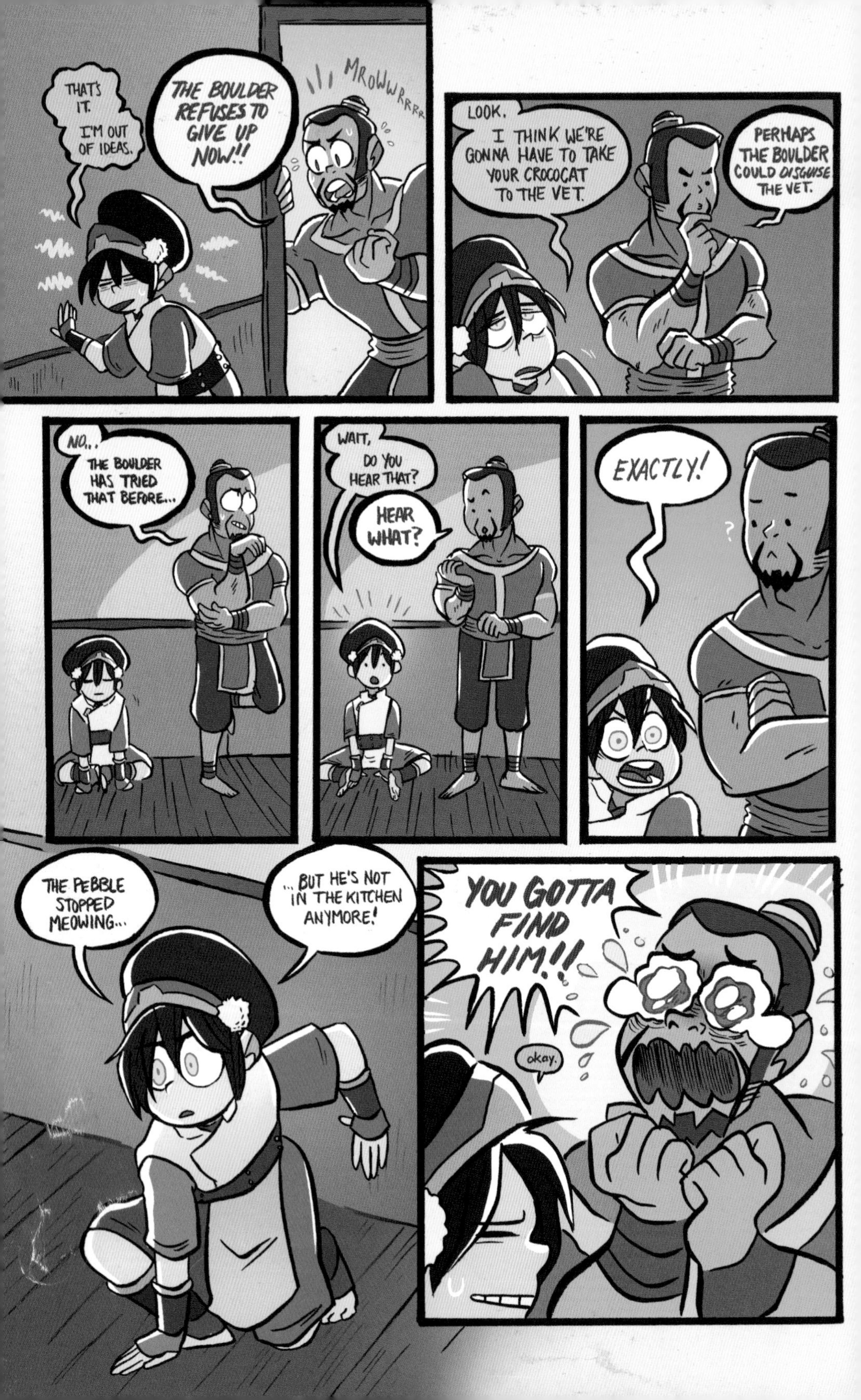

THAT'S IT. I'M OUT OF IDEAS.
THE BOULDER REFUSES TO GIVE UP NOW!!
MROWWRRRR
LOOK. I THINK WE'RE GONNA HAVE TO TAKE YOUR CROCOCAT TO THE VET.
PERHAPS THE BOULDER COULD DISGUISE THE VET.
NO... THE BOULDER HAS TRIED THAT BEFORE...
WAIT, DO YOU HEAR THAT?
HEAR WHAT?
EXACTLY!
THE PEBBLE STOPPED MEOWING...
...BUT HE'S NOT IN THE KITCHEN ANYMORE!
YOU GOTTA FIND HIM!!
okay.

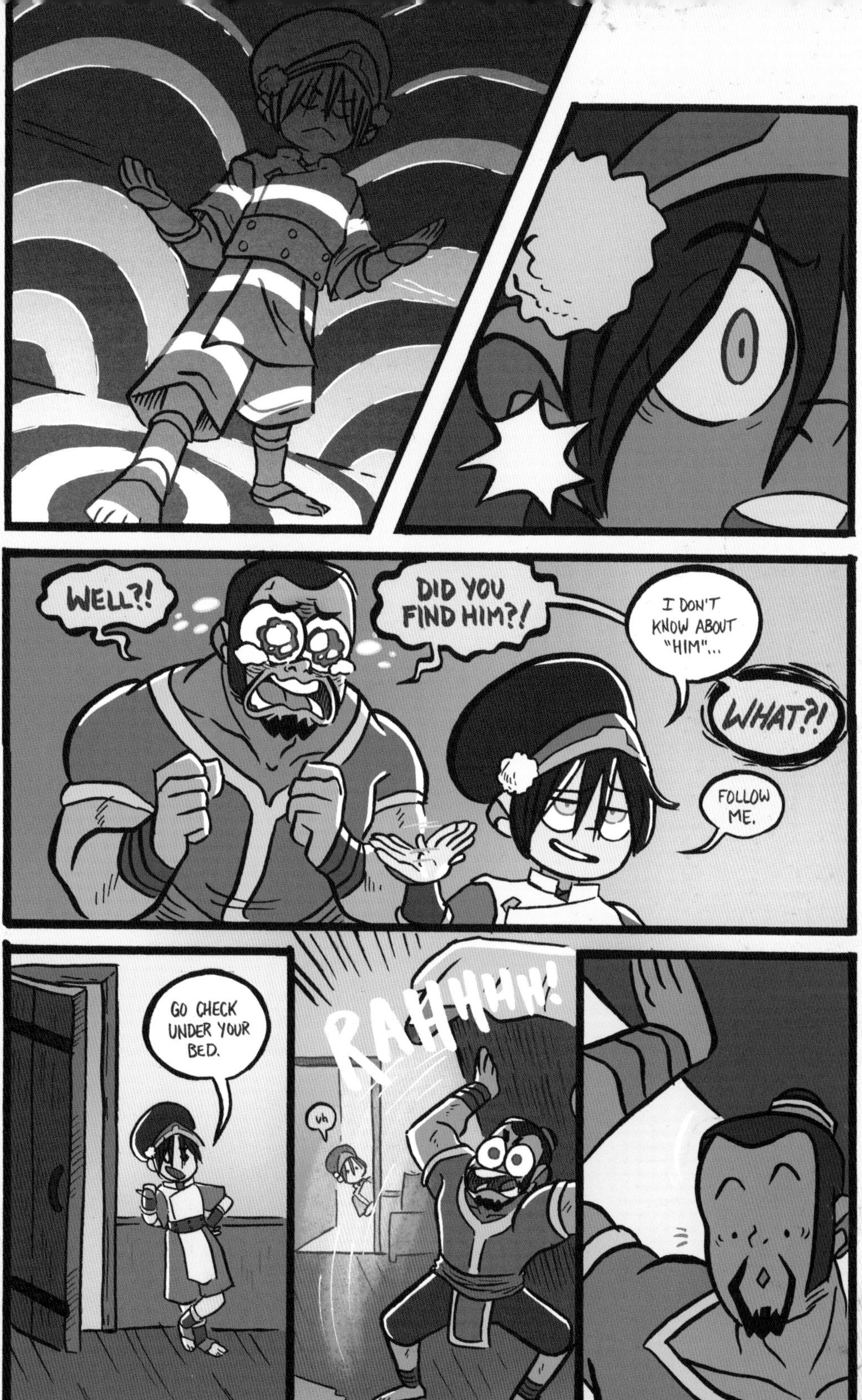
WELL?!
DID YOU FIND HIM?!
I DON'T KNOW ABOUT "HIM"...
WHAT?!
FOLLOW ME.
GO CHECK UNDER YOUR BED.
RAHHHH!
uh

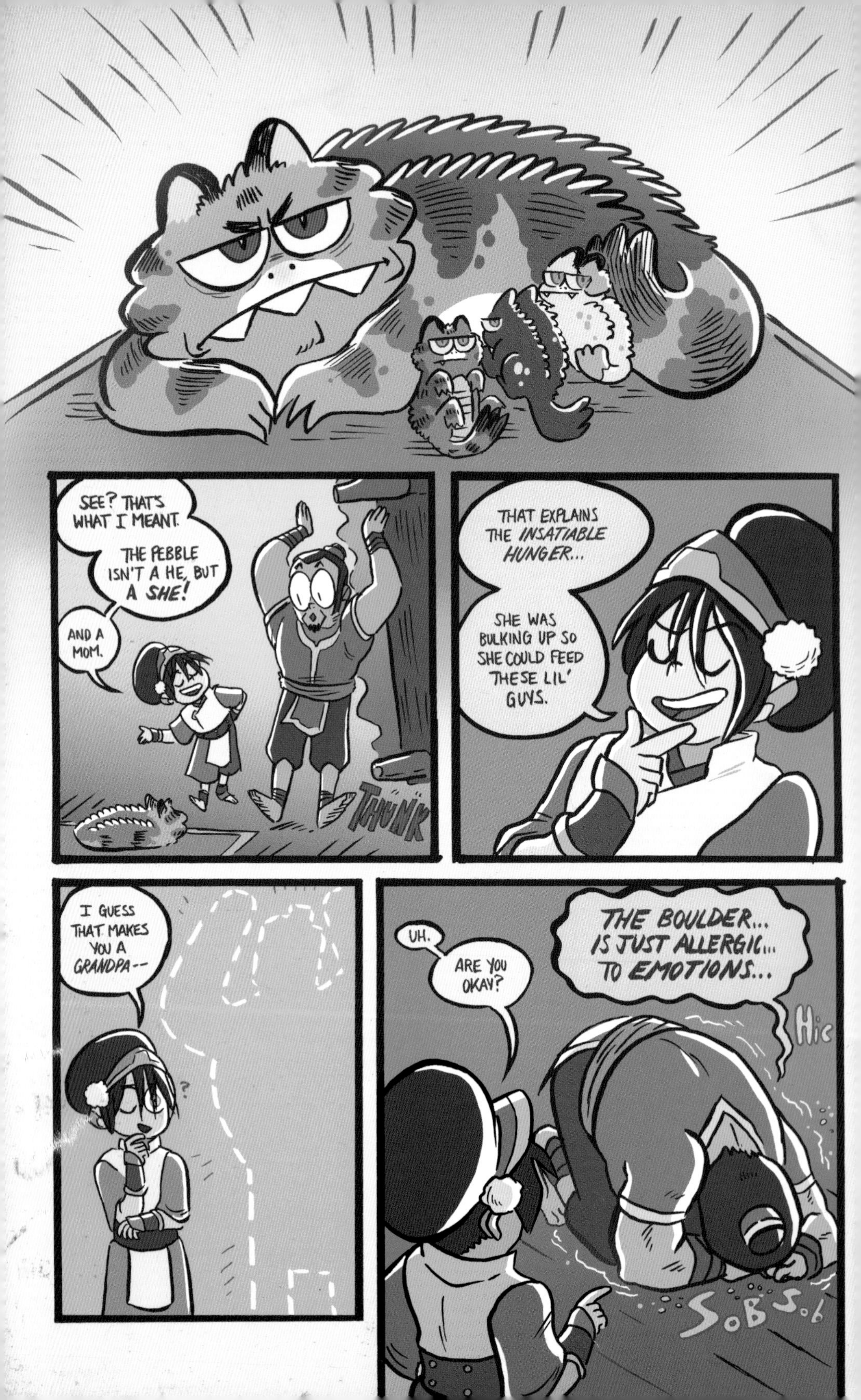
SEE? THAT'S WHAT I MEANT.
THE PEBBLE ISN'T A HE, BUT A SHE!
AND A MOM.
THUNK
THAT EXPLAINS THE INSATIABLE HUNGER...
SHE WAS BULKING UP SO SHE COULD FEED THESE LIL' GUYS.
I GUESS THAT MAKES YOU A GRANDPA--
?
UH.
ARE YOU OKAY?
THE BOULDER... IS JUST ALLERGIC... TO EMOTIONS...
Hic
SOB SOB

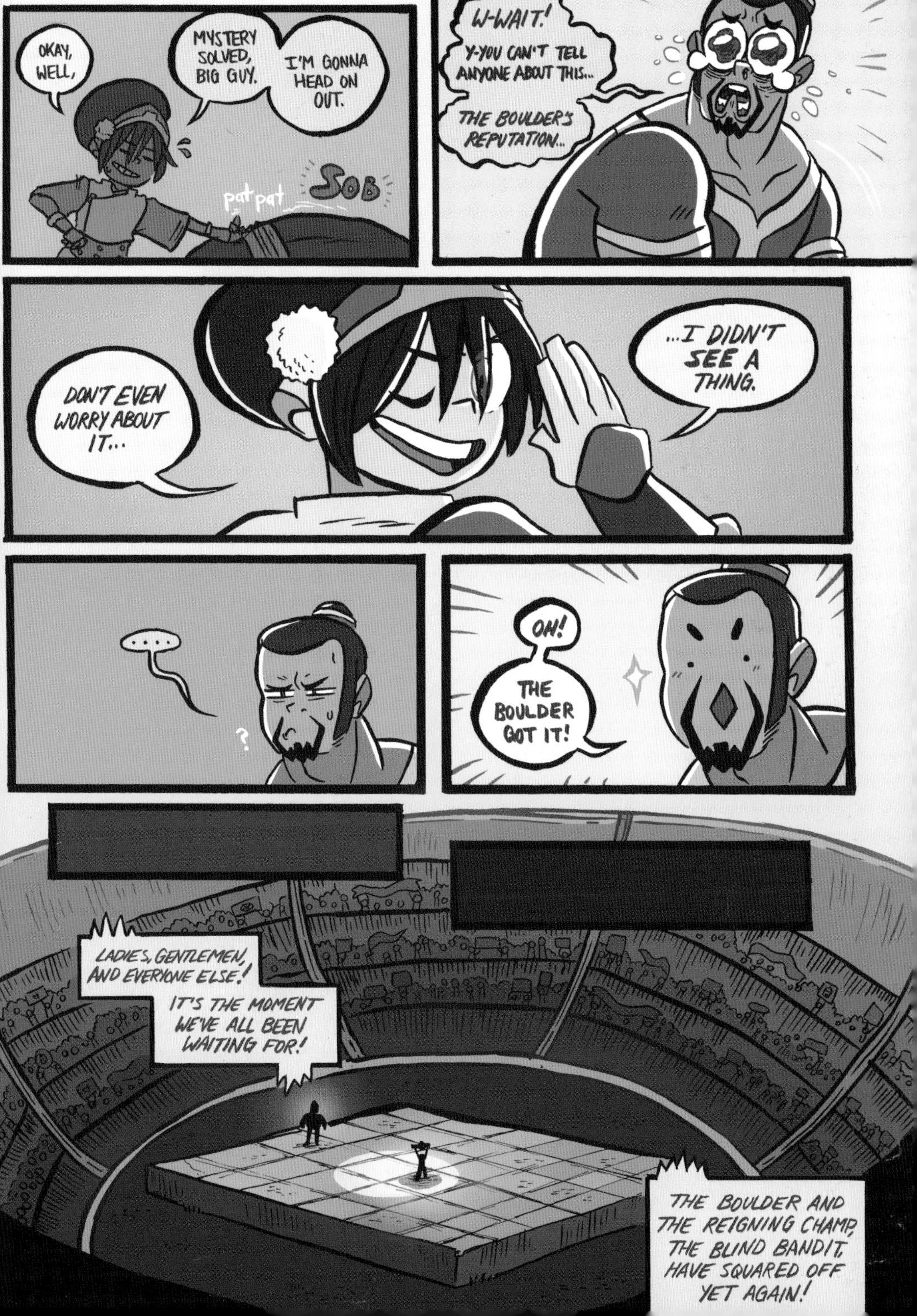
OKAY, WELL,
MYSTERY SOLVED, BIG GUY.
I'M GONNA HEAD ON OUT.
pat pat
SOB
W-WAIT!
Y-YOU CAN'T TELL ANYONE ABOUT THIS...
THE BOULDER'S REPUTATION...
DON'T EVEN WORRY ABOUT IT...
...I DIDN'T SEE A THING.
. . . .
?
OH!
THE BOULDER GOT IT!
[redacted]
[redacted]
LADIES, GENTLEMEN, AND EVERYONE ELSE!
IT'S THE MOMENT WE'VE ALL BEEN WAITING FOR!
THE BOULDER AND THE REIGNING CHAMP, THE BLIND BANDIT, HAVE SQUARED OFF YET AGAIN!

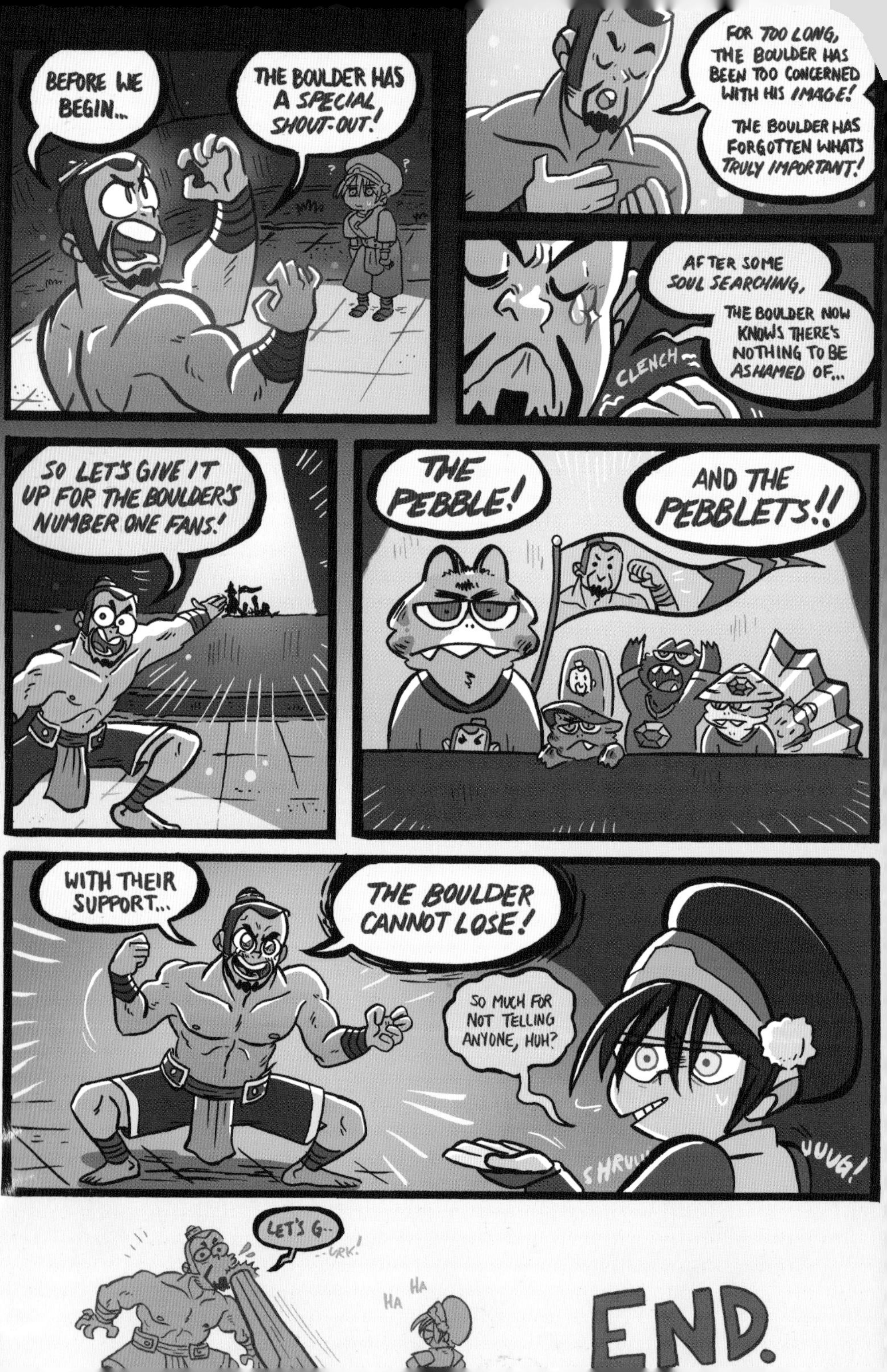
BEFORE WE BEGIN...
THE BOULDER HAS A SPECIAL SHOUT-OUT!
?
?
FOR TOO LONG, THE BOULDER HAS BEEN TOO CONCERNED WITH HIS IMAGE!
THE BOULDER HAS FORGOTTEN WHAT'S TRULY IMPORTANT!
AFTER SOME SOUL SEARCHING,
THE BOULDER NOW KNOWS THERE'S NOTHING TO BE ASHAMED OF...
CLENCH
SO LET'S GIVE IT UP FOR THE BOULDER'S NUMBER ONE FANS!
THE PEBBLE!
AND THE PEBBLETS!!
WITH THEIR SUPPORT...
THE BOULDER CANNOT LOSE!
SO MUCH FOR NOT TELLING ANYONE, HUH?
SHRUU
UUUG!
LET'S G...
...GRK!
HA
HA
END.

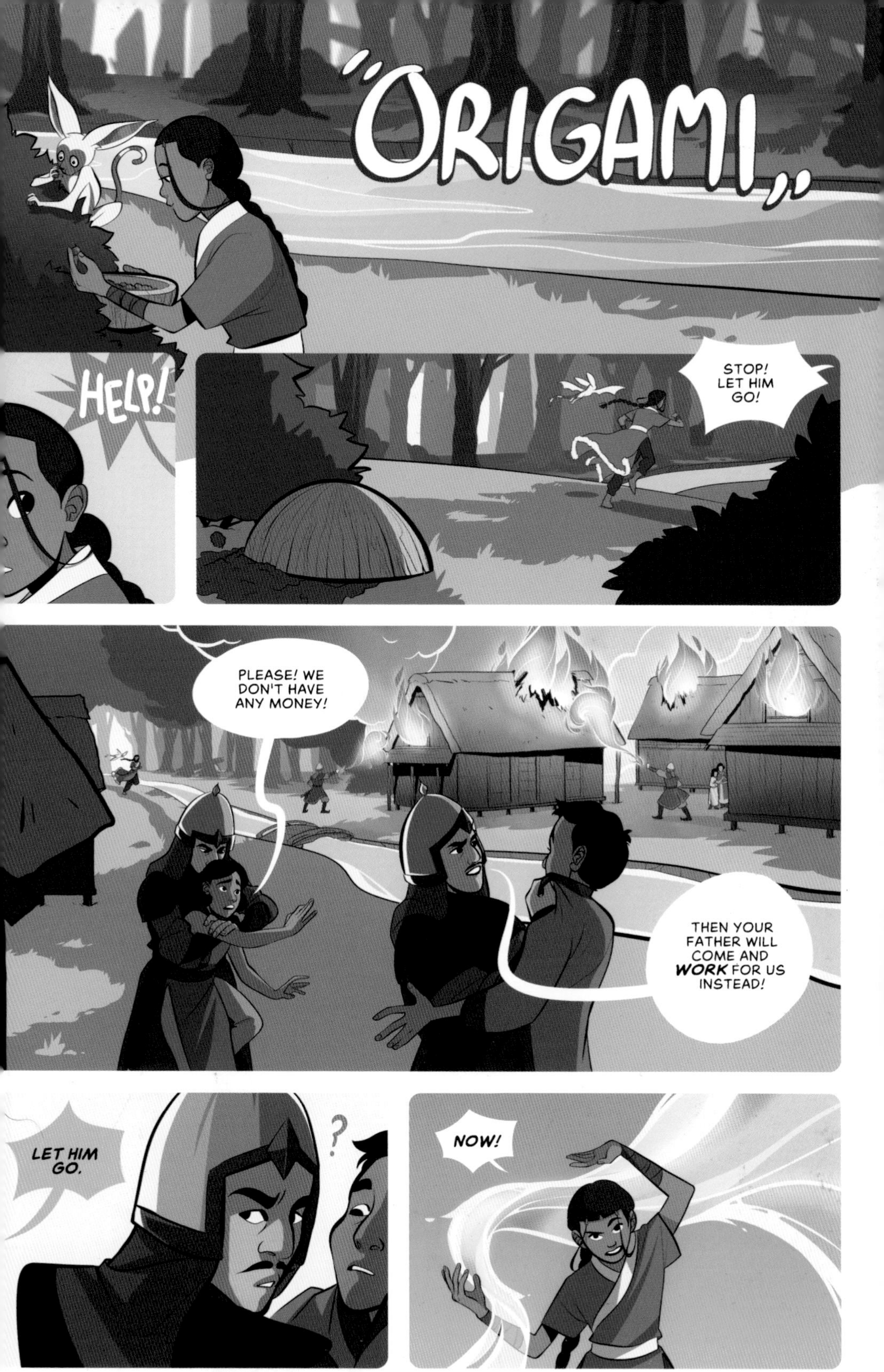
"ORIGAMI"
HELP!
STOP! LET HIM GO!
PLEASE! WE DON'T HAVE ANY MONEY!
THEN YOUR FATHER WILL COME AND WORK FOR US INSTEAD!
LET HIM GO.
?
NOW!

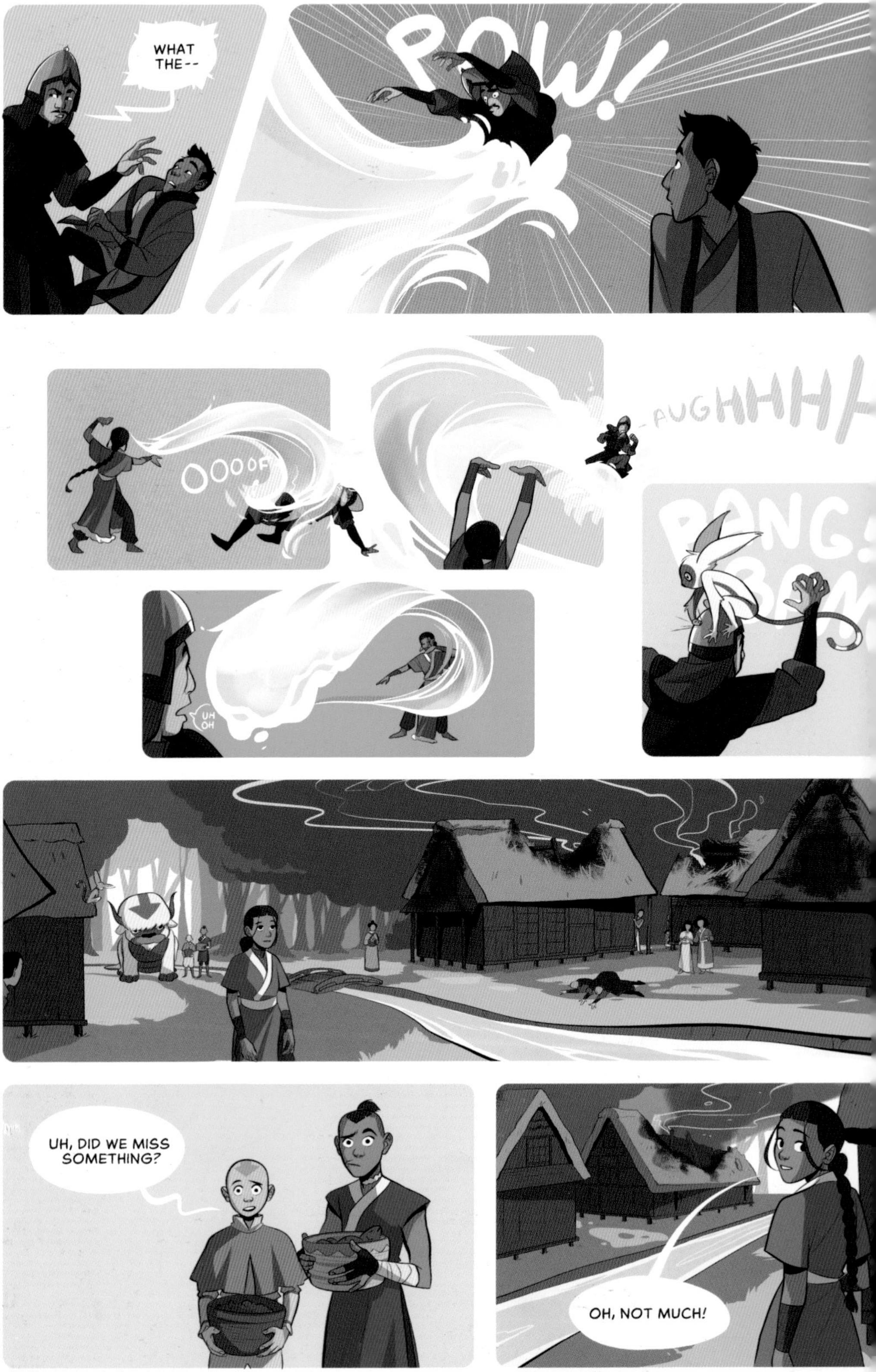
WHAT THE--
POW!
OOOOF
-AUGHHHH
UH OH
BANG!
UH, DID WE MISS SOMETHING?
OH, NOT MUCH!

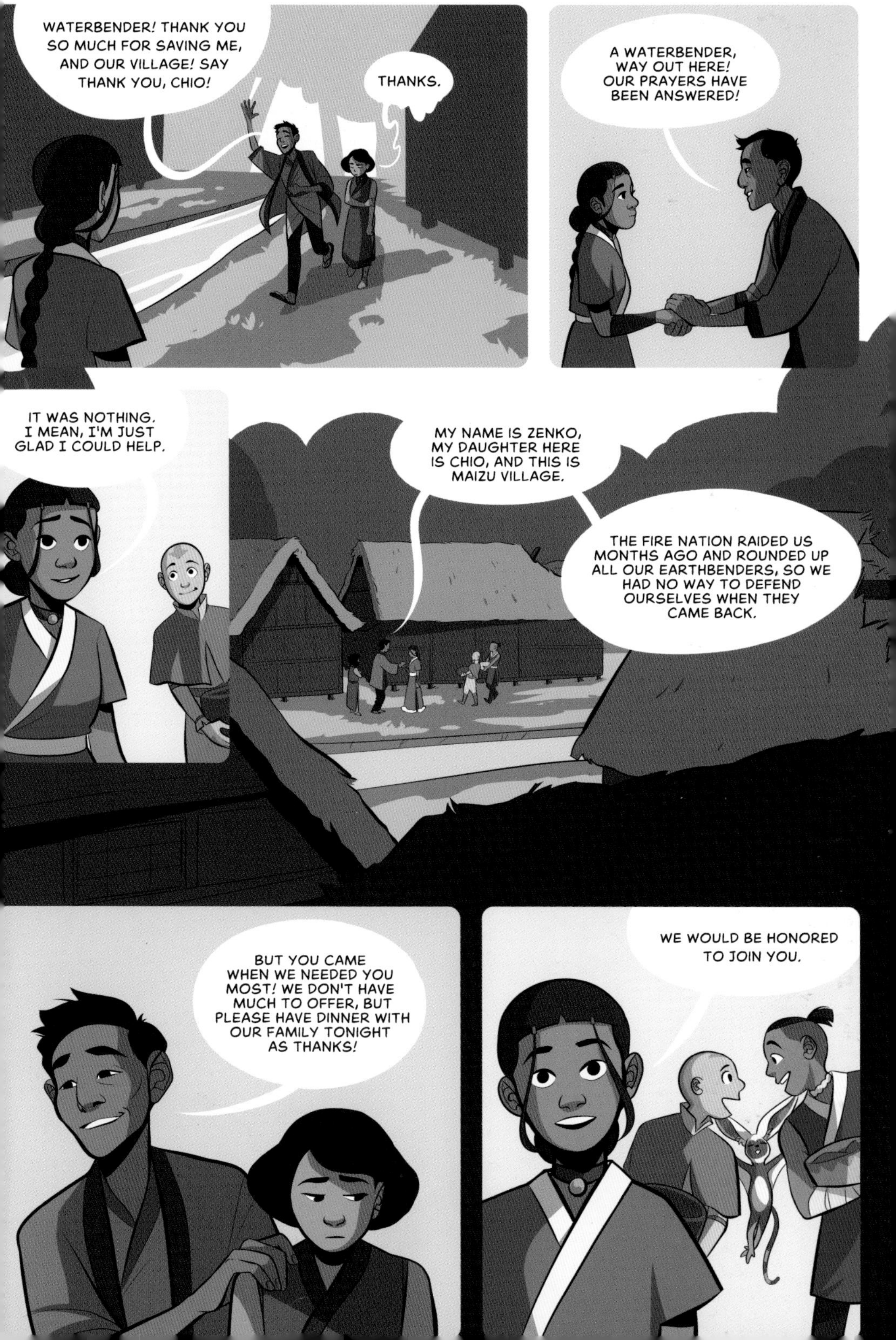
WATERBENDER! THANK YOU SO MUCH FOR SAVING ME, AND OUR VILLAGE! SAY THANK YOU, CHIO!
THANKS.
A WATERBENDER, WAY OUT HERE! OUR PRAYERS HAVE BEEN ANSWERED!
IT WAS NOTHING. I MEAN, I'M JUST GLAD I COULD HELP.
MY NAME IS ZENKO, MY DAUGHTER HERE IS CHIO, AND THIS IS MAIZU VILLAGE.
THE FIRE NATION RAIDED US MONTHS AGO AND ROUNDED UP ALL OUR EARTHBENDERS, SO WE HAD NO WAY TO DEFEND OURSELVES WHEN THEY CAME BACK.
BUT YOU CAME WHEN WE NEEDED YOU MOST! WE DON'T HAVE MUCH TO OFFER, BUT PLEASE HAVE DINNER WITH OUR FAMILY TONIGHT AS THANKS!
WE WOULD BE HONORED TO JOIN YOU.

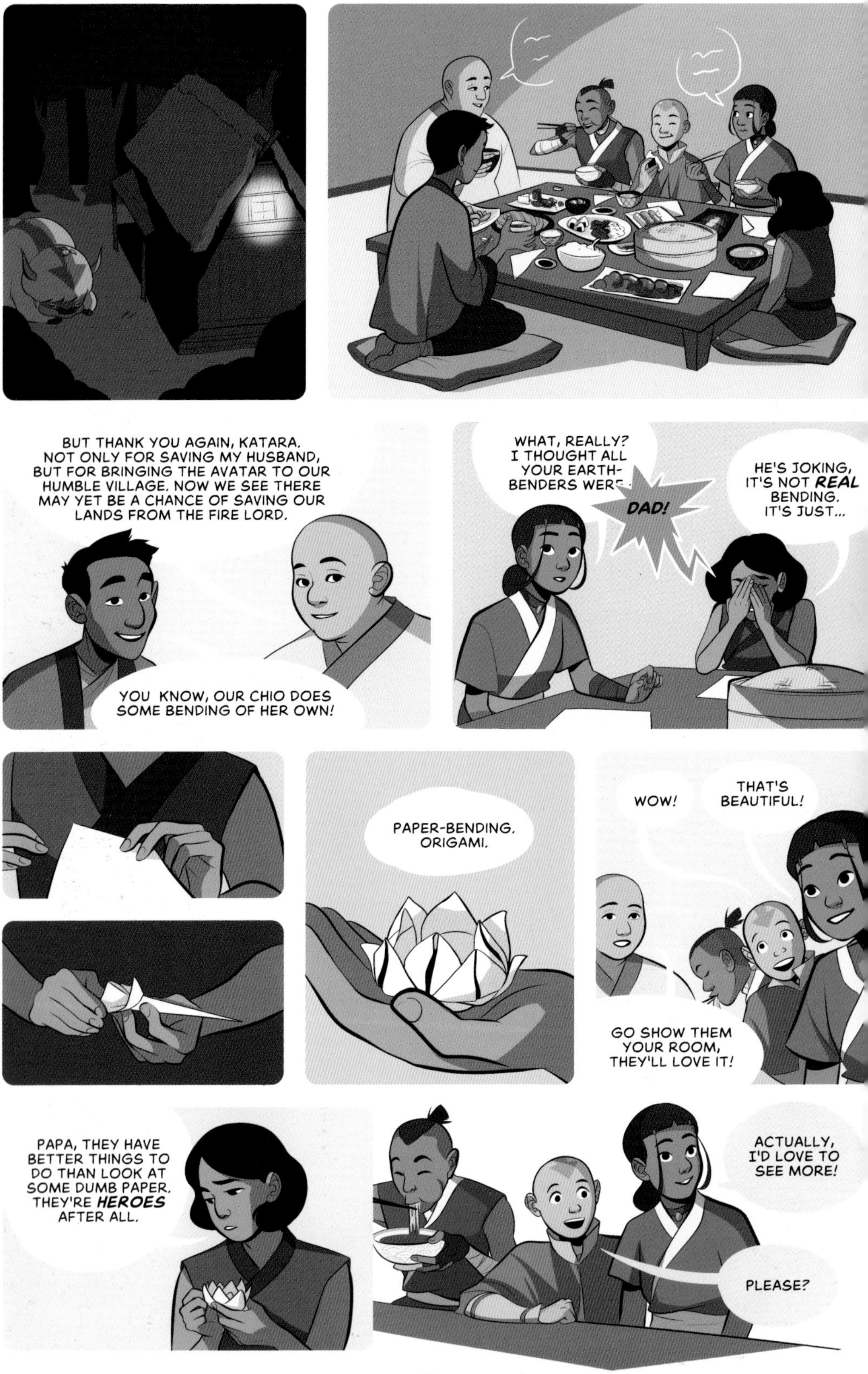
BUT THANK YOU AGAIN, KATARA. NOT ONLY FOR SAVING MY HUSBAND, BUT FOR BRINGING THE AVATAR TO OUR HUMBLE VILLAGE. NOW WE SEE THERE MAY YET BE A CHANCE OF SAVING OUR LANDS FROM THE FIRE LORD.
YOU KNOW, OUR CHIO DOES SOME BENDING OF HER OWN!
WHAT, REALLY? I THOUGHT ALL YOUR EARTH-BENDERS WERE-
DAD!
HE'S JOKING, IT'S NOT REAL BENDING. IT'S JUST...
PAPER-BENDING. ORIGAMI.
WOW!
THAT'S BEAUTIFUL!
GO SHOW THEM YOUR ROOM, THEY'LL LOVE IT!
PAPA, THEY HAVE BETTER THINGS TO DO THAN LOOK AT SOME DUMB PAPER. THEY'RE HEROES AFTER ALL.
ACTUALLY, I'D LOVE TO SEE MORE!
PLEASE?

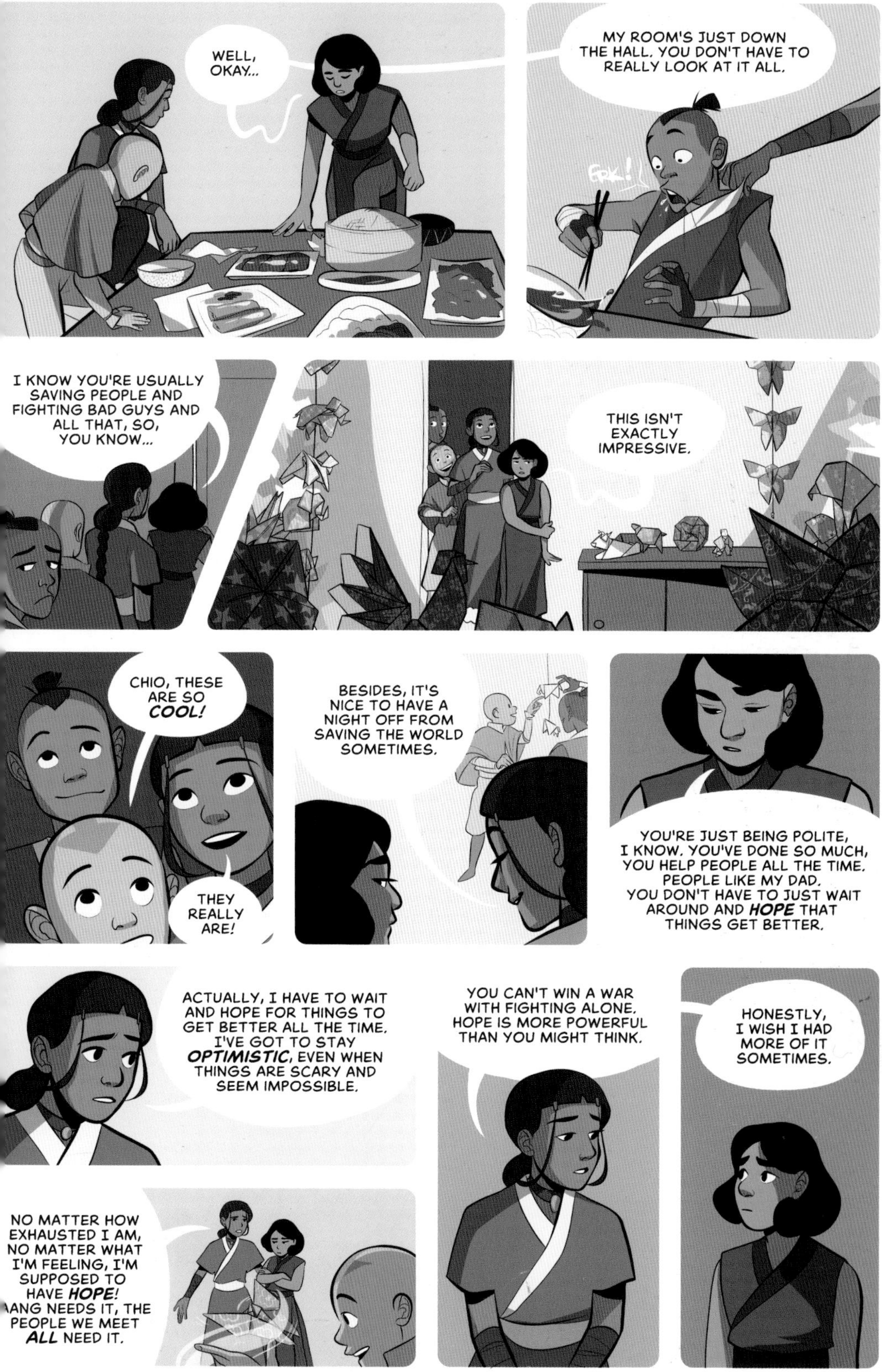
WELL, OKAY...
MY ROOM'S JUST DOWN THE HALL. YOU DON'T HAVE TO REALLY LOOK AT IT ALL.
ERK!
I KNOW YOU'RE USUALLY SAVING PEOPLE AND FIGHTING BAD GUYS AND ALL THAT, SO, YOU KNOW...
THIS ISN'T EXACTLY IMPRESSIVE.
CHIO, THESE ARE SO ***COOL!***
THEY REALLY ARE!
BESIDES, IT'S NICE TO HAVE A NIGHT OFF FROM SAVING THE WORLD SOMETIMES.
YOU'RE JUST BEING POLITE, I KNOW. YOU'VE DONE SO MUCH, YOU HELP PEOPLE ALL THE TIME. PEOPLE LIKE MY DAD. YOU DON'T HAVE TO JUST WAIT AROUND AND ***HOPE*** THAT THINGS GET BETTER.
ACTUALLY, I HAVE TO WAIT AND HOPE FOR THINGS TO GET BETTER ALL THE TIME. I'VE GOT TO STAY ***OPTIMISTIC***, EVEN WHEN THINGS ARE SCARY AND SEEM IMPOSSIBLE.
NO MATTER HOW EXHAUSTED I AM, NO MATTER WHAT I'M FEELING, I'M SUPPOSED TO HAVE ***HOPE***! ANG NEEDS IT, THE PEOPLE WE MEET ***ALL*** NEED IT.
YOU CAN'T WIN A WAR WITH FIGHTING ALONE. HOPE IS MORE POWERFUL THAN YOU MIGHT THINK.
HONESTLY, I WISH I HAD MORE OF IT SOMETIMES.

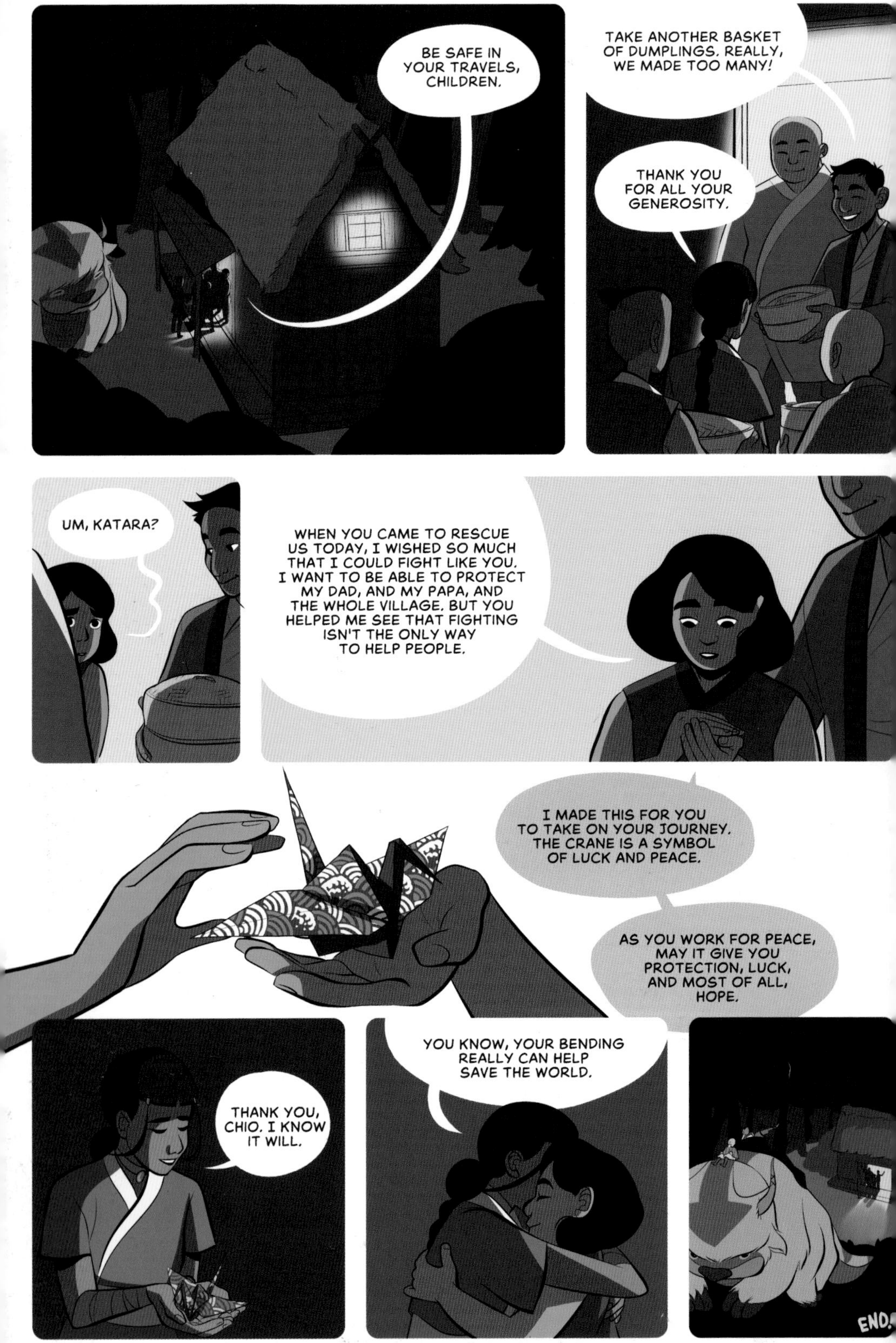
BE SAFE IN YOUR TRAVELS, CHILDREN.
TAKE ANOTHER BASKET OF DUMPLINGS. REALLY, WE MADE TOO MANY!
THANK YOU FOR ALL YOUR GENEROSITY.
UM, KATARA?
WHEN YOU CAME TO RESCUE US TODAY, I WISHED SO MUCH THAT I COULD FIGHT LIKE YOU. I WANT TO BE ABLE TO PROTECT MY DAD, AND MY PAPA, AND THE WHOLE VILLAGE. BUT YOU HELPED ME SEE THAT FIGHTING ISN'T THE ONLY WAY TO HELP PEOPLE.
I MADE THIS FOR YOU TO TAKE ON YOUR JOURNEY. THE CRANE IS A SYMBOL OF LUCK AND PEACE.
AS YOU WORK FOR PEACE, MAY IT GIVE YOU PROTECTION, LUCK, AND MOST OF ALL, HOPE.
THANK YOU, CHIO. I KNOW IT WILL.
YOU KNOW, YOUR BENDING REALLY CAN HELP SAVE THE WORLD.
END.

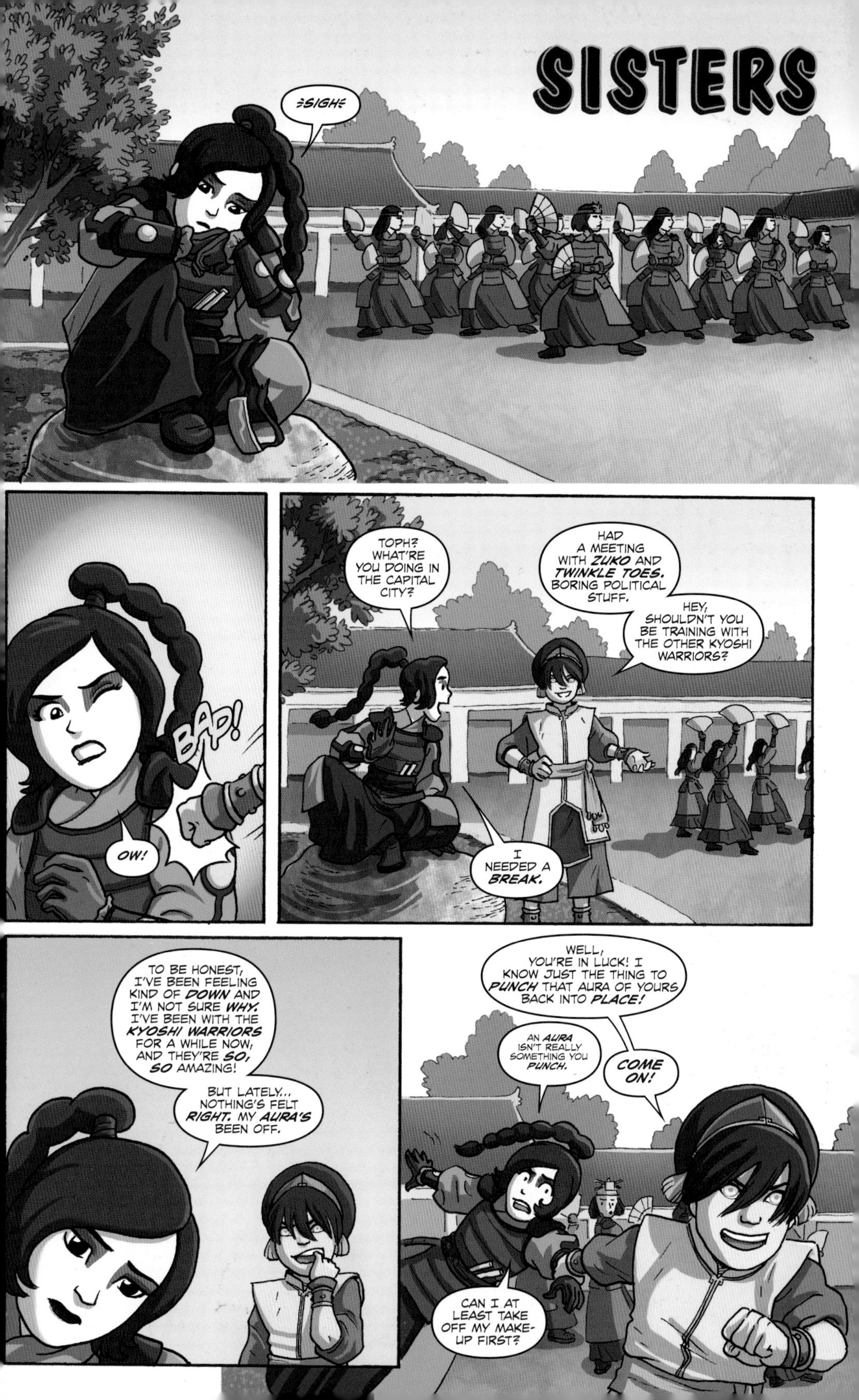
SISTERS
SIGH
BAP!
OW!
TOPH? WHAT'RE YOU DOING IN THE CAPITAL CITY?
HAD A MEETING WITH ZUKO AND TWINKLE TOES. BORING POLITICAL STUFF.
HEY, SHOULDN'T YOU BE TRAINING WITH THE OTHER KYOSHI WARRIORS?
I NEEDED A BREAK.
TO BE HONEST, I'VE BEEN FEELING KIND OF DOWN AND I'M NOT SURE WHY. I'VE BEEN WITH THE KYOSHI WARRIORS FOR A WHILE NOW, AND THEY'RE SO, SO AMAZING!
BUT LATELY... NOTHING'S FELT RIGHT. MY AURA'S BEEN OFF.
WELL, YOU'RE IN LUCK! I KNOW JUST THE THING TO PUNCH THAT AURA OF YOURS BACK INTO PLACE!
AN AURA ISN'T REALLY SOMETHING YOU PUNCH.
COME ON!
CAN I AT LEAST TAKE OFF MY MAKE-UP FIRST?

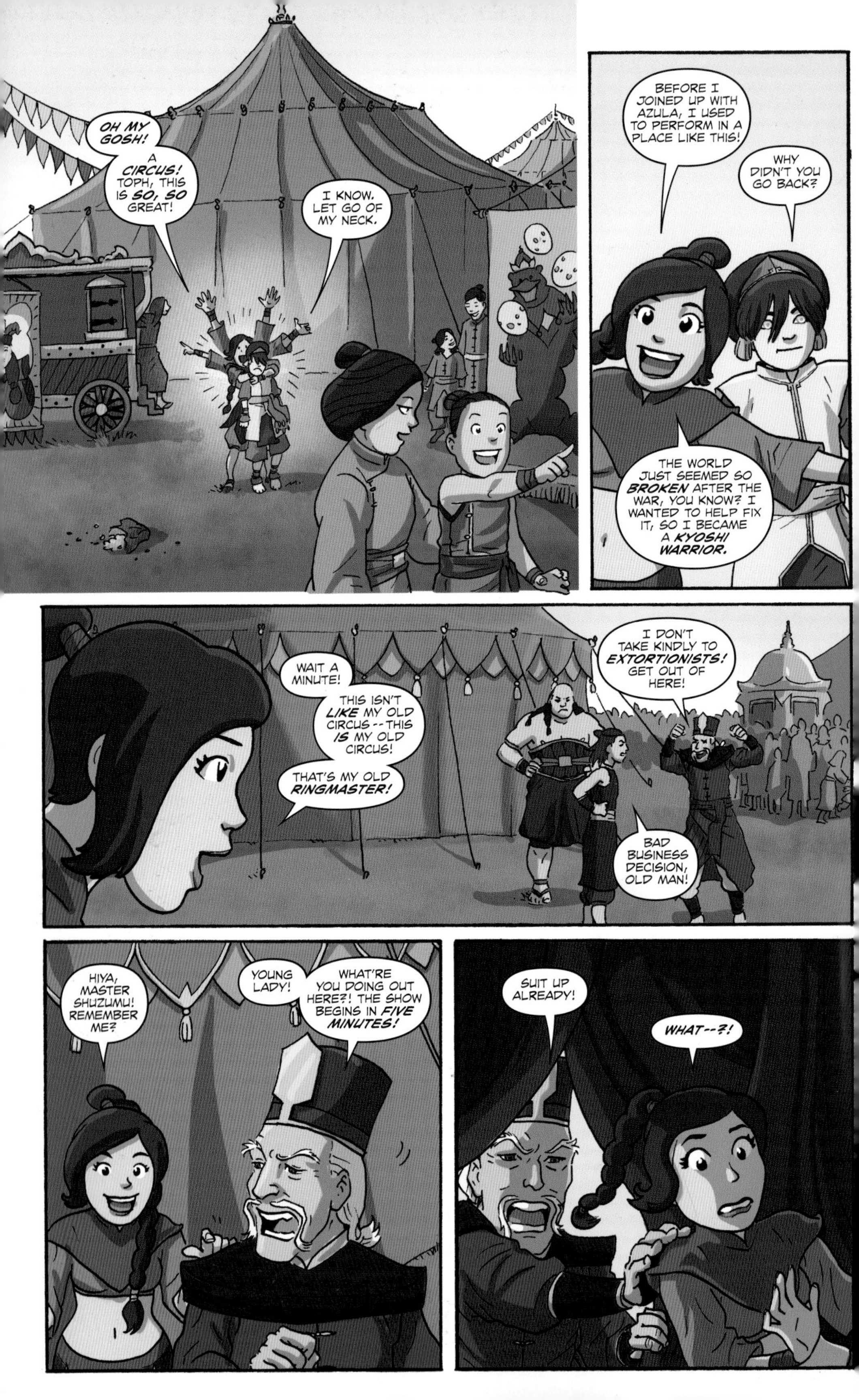
OH MY GOSH!
A CIRCUS! TOPH, THIS IS SO, SO GREAT!
I KNOW. LET GO OF MY NECK.
BEFORE I JOINED UP WITH AZULA, I USED TO PERFORM IN A PLACE LIKE THIS!
WHY DIDN'T YOU GO BACK?
THE WORLD JUST SEEMED SO BROKEN AFTER THE WAR, YOU KNOW? I WANTED TO HELP FIX IT, SO I BECAME A KYOSHI WARRIOR.
WAIT A MINUTE!
THIS ISN'T LIKE MY OLD CIRCUS--THIS IS MY OLD CIRCUS!
THAT'S MY OLD RINGMASTER!
I DON'T TAKE KINDLY TO EXTORTIONISTS! GET OUT OF HERE!
BAD BUSINESS DECISION, OLD MAN!
HIYA, MASTER SHUZUMU! REMEMBER ME?
YOUNG LADY!
WHAT'RE YOU DOING OUT HERE?! THE SHOW BEGINS IN FIVE MINUTES!
SUIT UP ALREADY!
WHAT--?!

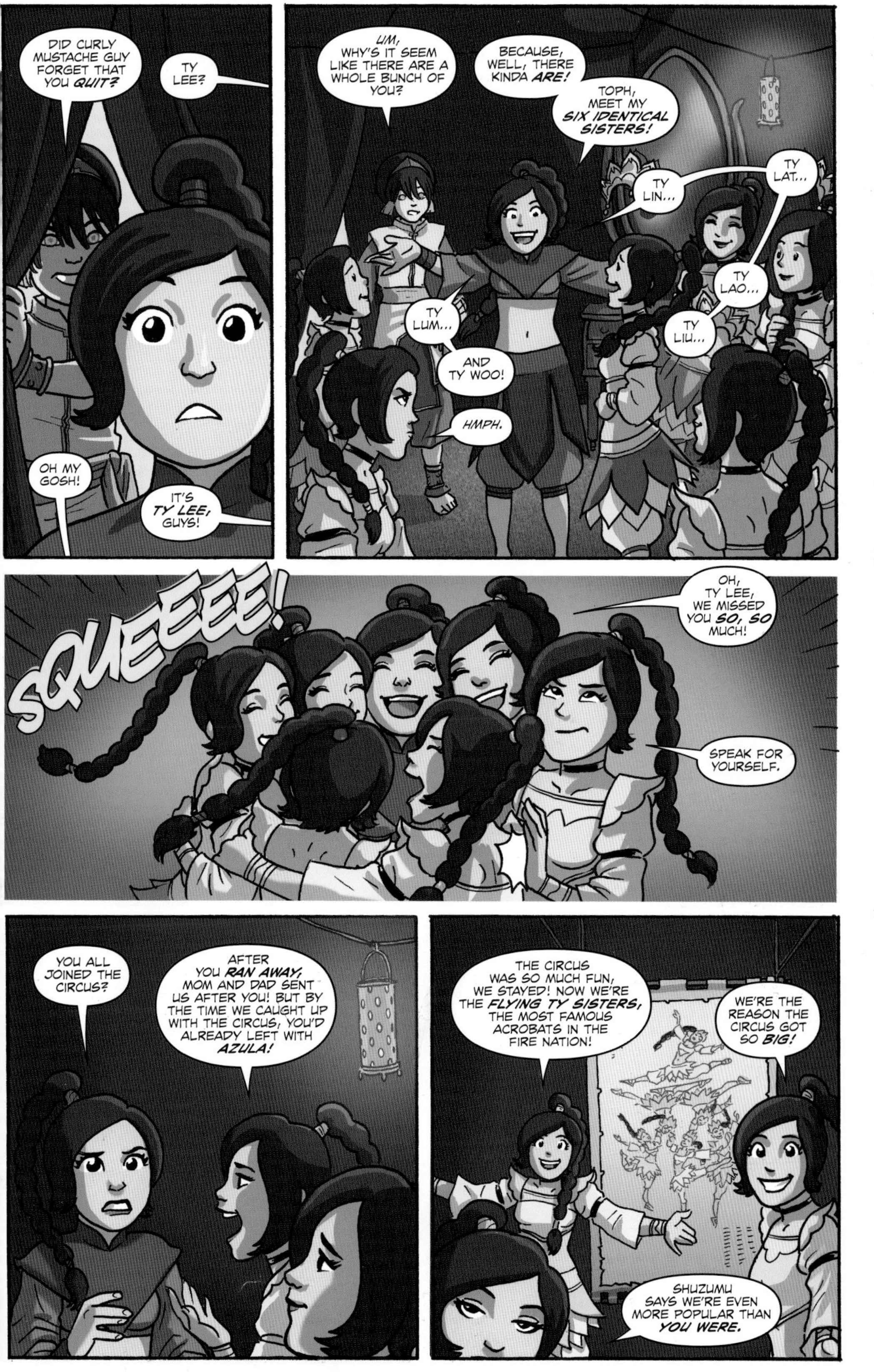
DID CURLY MUSTACHE GUY FORGET THAT YOU QUIT?
TY LEE?
OH MY GOSH!
IT'S TY LEE, GUYS!
UM, WHY'S IT SEEM LIKE THERE ARE A WHOLE BUNCH OF YOU?
BECAUSE, WELL, THERE KINDA ARE!
TOPH, MEET MY SIX IDENTICAL SISTERS!
TY LIN...
TY LAT...
TY LAO...
TY LIU...
TY LUM...
AND TY WOO!
HMPH.
SQUEEEEE!
OH, TY LEE, WE MISSED YOU SO, SO MUCH!
SPEAK FOR YOURSELF.
YOU ALL JOINED THE CIRCUS?
AFTER YOU RAN AWAY, MOM AND DAD SENT US AFTER YOU! BUT BY THE TIME WE CAUGHT UP WITH THE CIRCUS, YOU'D ALREADY LEFT WITH AZULA!
THE CIRCUS WAS SO MUCH FUN, WE STAYED! NOW WE'RE THE FLYING TY SISTERS, THE MOST FAMOUS ACROBATS IN THE FIRE NATION!
WE'RE THE REASON THE CIRCUS GOT SO BIG!
SHUZUMU SAYS WE'RE EVEN MORE POPULAR THAN YOU WERE.

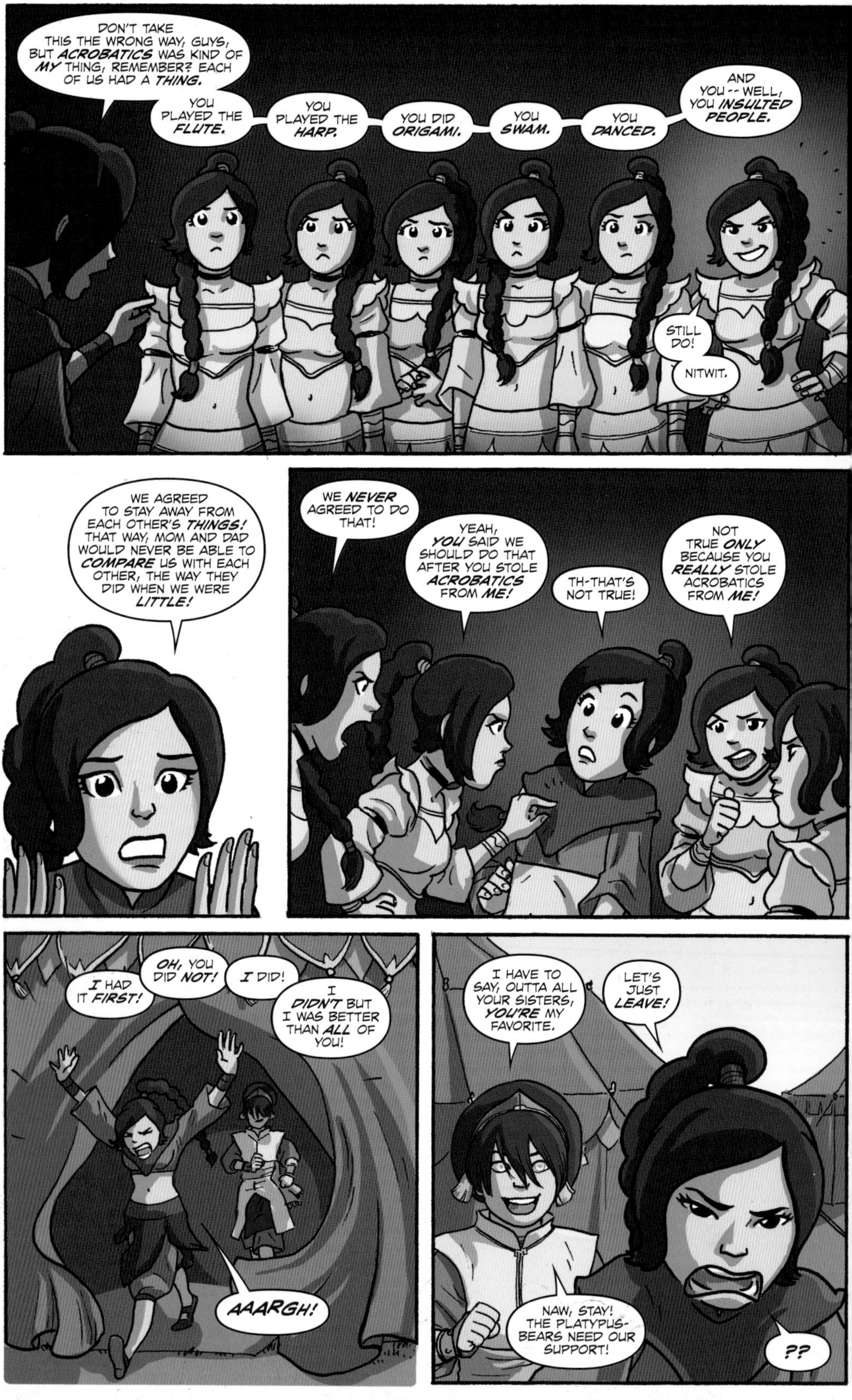

DON'T TAKE THIS THE WRONG WAY, GUYS, BUT ACROBATICS WAS KIND OF MY THING, REMEMBER? EACH OF US HAD A THING.
YOU PLAYED THE FLUTE.
YOU PLAYED THE HARP.
YOU DID ORIGAMI.
YOU SWAM.
YOU DANCED.
AND YOU -- WELL, YOU INSULTED PEOPLE.
STILL DO!
NITWIT.
WE AGREED TO STAY AWAY FROM EACH OTHER'S THINGS! THAT WAY, MOM AND DAD WOULD NEVER BE ABLE TO COMPARE US WITH EACH OTHER, THE WAY THEY DID WHEN WE WERE LITTLE!
WE NEVER AGREED TO DO THAT!
YEAH, YOU SAID WE SHOULD DO THAT AFTER YOU STOLE ACROBATICS FROM ME!
TH-THAT'S NOT TRUE!
NOT TRUE ONLY BECAUSE YOU REALLY STOLE ACROBATICS FROM ME!
I HAD IT FIRST!
OH, YOU DID NOT!
I DID!
I DIDN'T BUT I WAS BETTER THAN ALL OF YOU!
AAARGH!
I HAVE TO SAY, OUTTA ALL YOUR SISTERS, YOU'RE MY FAVORITE.
LET'S JUST LEAVE!
NAW, STAY! THE PLATYPUS-BEARS NEED OUR SUPPORT!
??

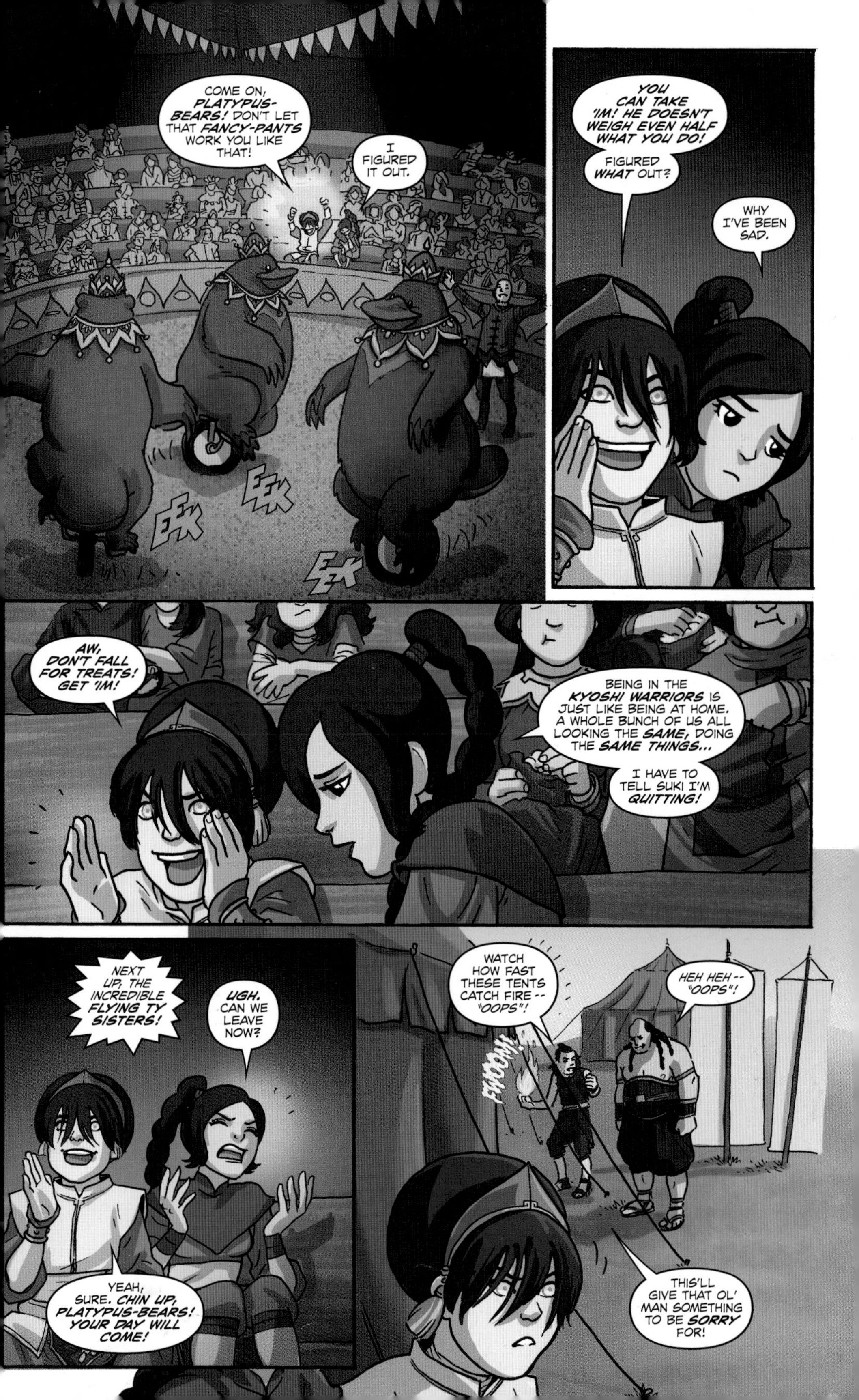

COME ON, PLATYPUS-BEARS! DON'T LET THAT FANCY-PANTS WORK YOU LIKE THAT!
I FIGURED IT OUT.
EEK
EEK
EEK
YOU CAN TAKE 'IM! HE DOESN'T WEIGH EVEN HALF WHAT YOU DO!
FIGURED WHAT OUT?
WHY I'VE BEEN SAD.
AW, DON'T FALL FOR TREATS! GET 'IM!
BEING IN THE KYOSHI WARRIORS IS JUST LIKE BEING AT HOME. A WHOLE BUNCH OF US ALL LOOKING THE SAME, DOING THE SAME THINGS...
I HAVE TO TELL SUKI I'M QUITTING!
NEXT UP, THE INCREDIBLE FLYING TY SISTERS!
UGH. CAN WE LEAVE NOW?
YEAH, SURE. CHIN UP, PLATYPUS-BEARS! YOUR DAY WILL COME!
WATCH HOW FAST THESE TENTS CATCH FIRE-- "OOPS"!
HEH HEH-- "OOPS"!
THIS'LL GIVE THAT OL' MAN SOMETHING TO BE SORRY FOR!

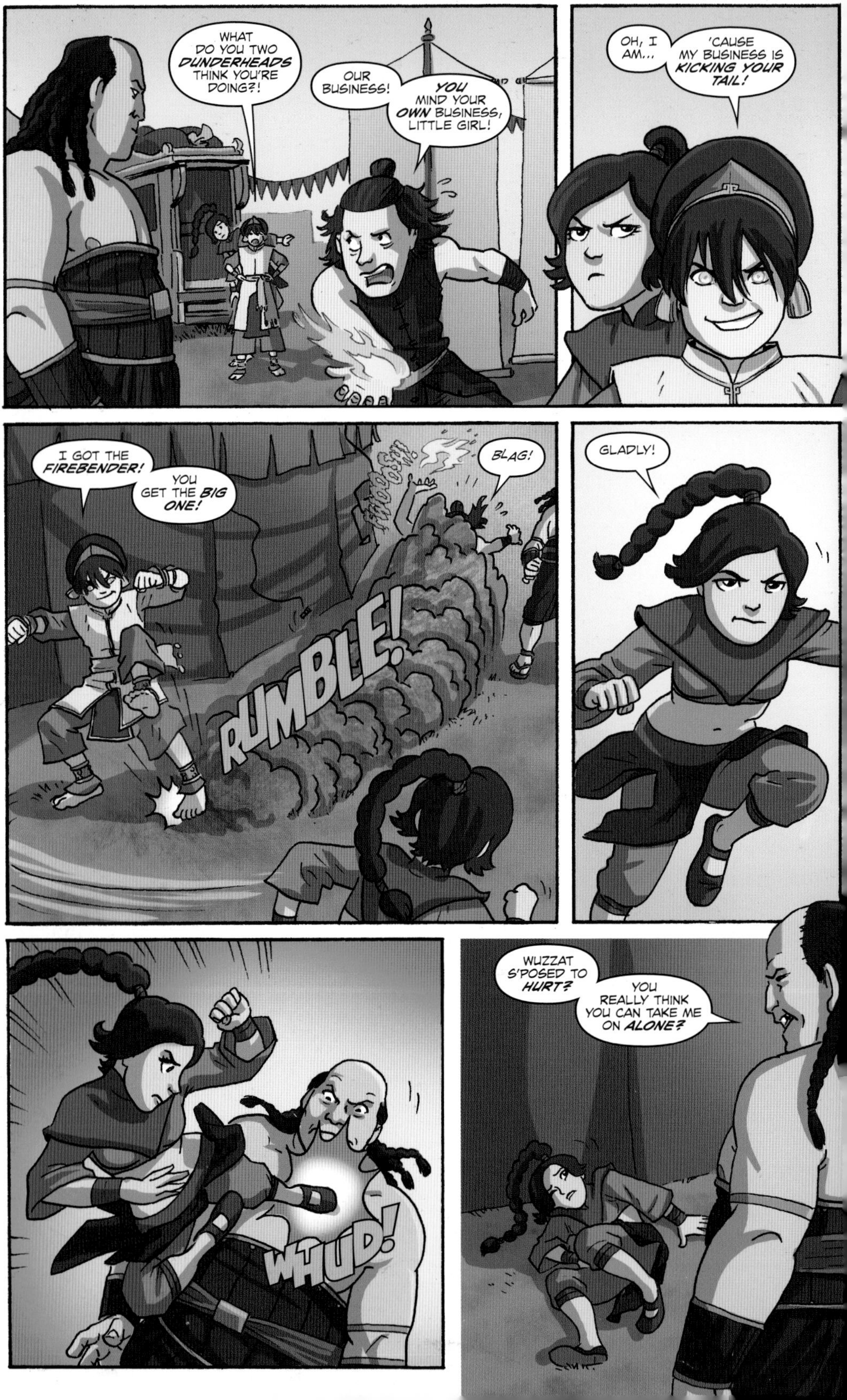
WHAT DO YOU TWO DUNDERHEADS THINK YOU'RE DOING?!
OUR BUSINESS!
YOU MIND YOUR OWN BUSINESS, LITTLE GIRL!
OH, I AM...
'CAUSE MY BUSINESS IS KICKING YOUR TAIL!
I GOT THE FIREBENDER!
YOU GET THE BIG ONE!
BLAG!
RUMBLE!
GLADLY!
WHUD!
WUZZAT S'POSED TO HURT?
YOU REALLY THINK YOU CAN TAKE ME ON ALONE?

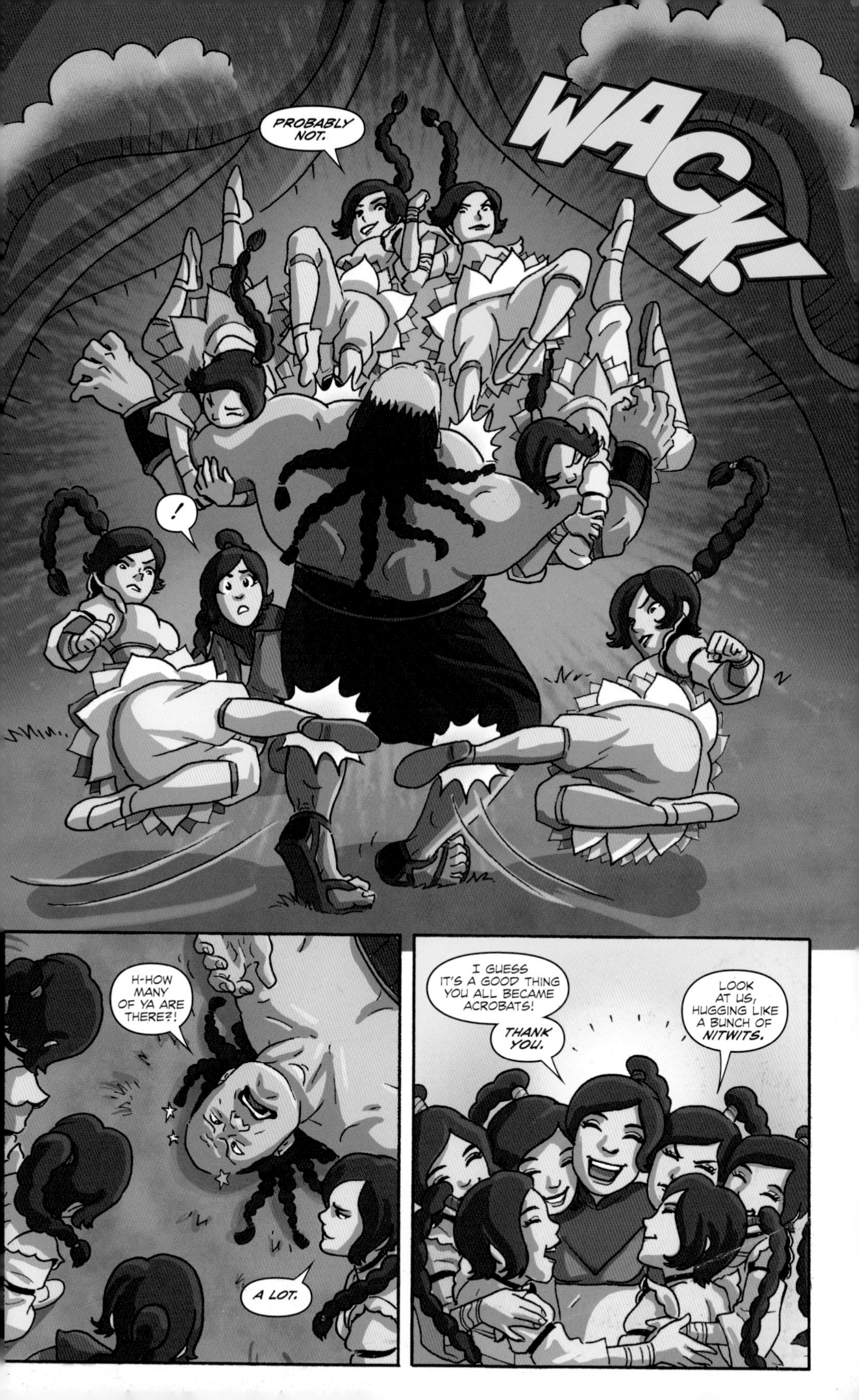
PROBABLY NOT.
WACK!
!
H-HOW MANY OF YA ARE THERE?!
A LOT.
I GUESS IT'S A GOOD THING YOU ALL BECAME ACROBATS!
THANK YOU.
LOOK AT US, HUGGING LIKE A BUNCH OF NITWITS.

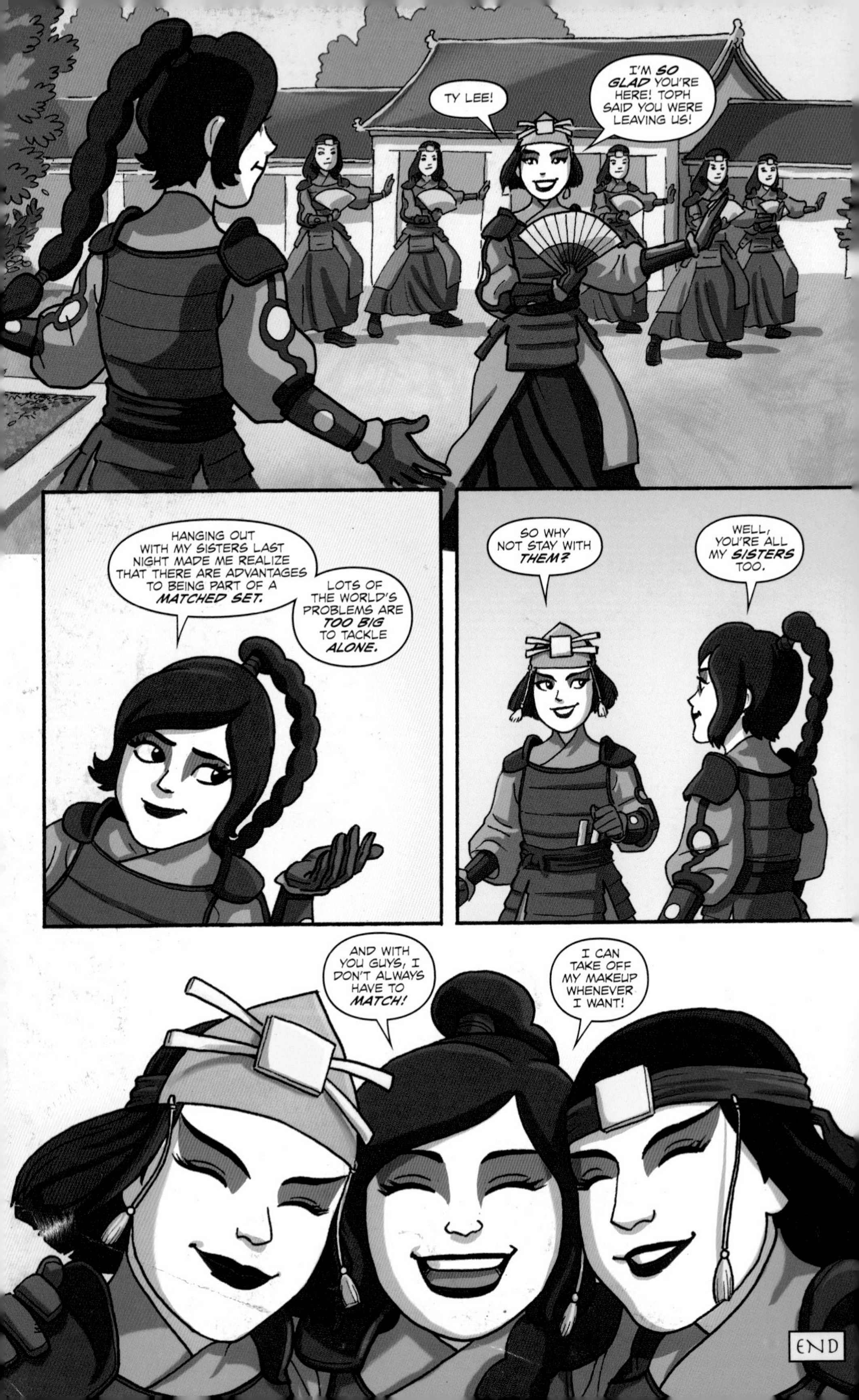
TY LEE!
I'M SO GLAD YOU'RE HERE! TOPH SAID YOU WERE LEAVING US!
HANGING OUT WITH MY SISTERS LAST NIGHT MADE ME REALIZE THAT THERE ARE ADVANTAGES TO BEING PART OF A MATCHED SET.
LOTS OF THE WORLD'S PROBLEMS ARE TOO BIG TO TACKLE ALONE.
SO WHY NOT STAY WITH THEM?
WELL, YOU'RE ALL MY SISTERS TOO.
AND WITH YOU GUYS, I DON'T ALWAYS HAVE TO MATCH!
I CAN TAKE OFF MY MAKEUP WHENEVER I WANT!
END

THE SCARECROW

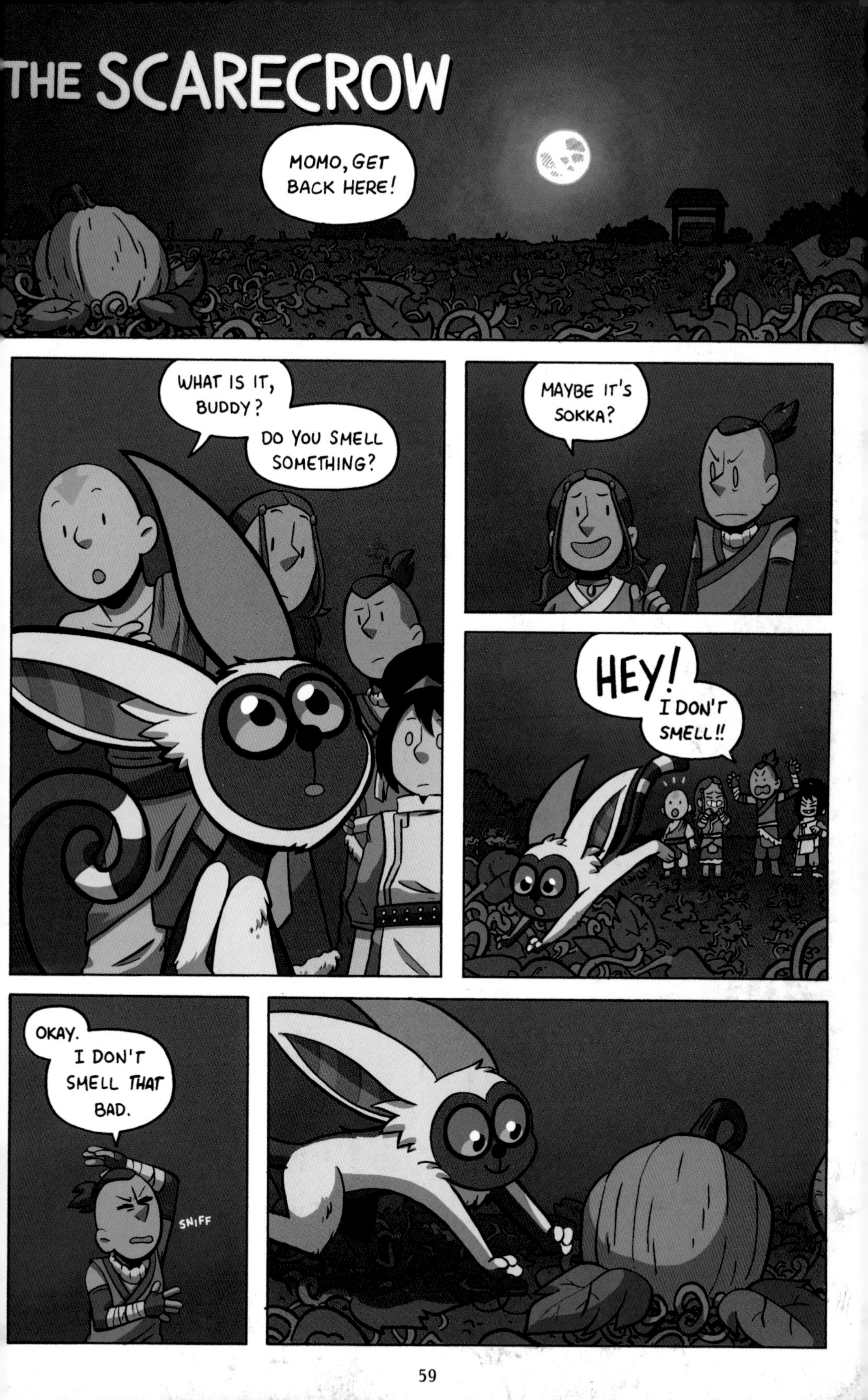
MOMO, GET BACK HERE!
WHAT IS IT, BUDDY?
DO YOU SMELL SOMETHING?
MAYBE IT'S SOKKA?
HEY!
I DON'T SMELL!!
OKAY. I DON'T SMELL THAT BAD.
SNIFF

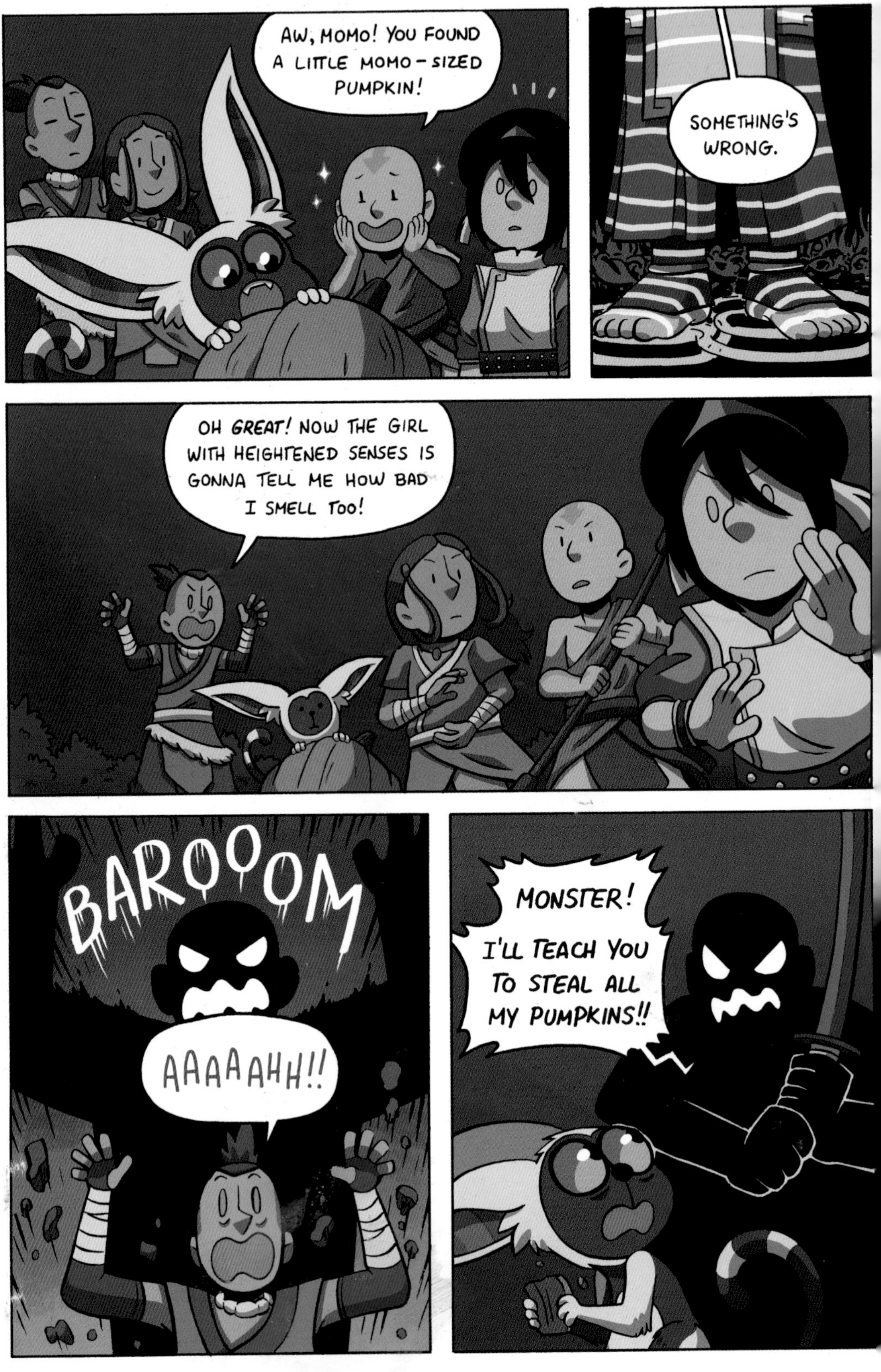
AW, MOMO! YOU FOUND A LITTLE MOMO-SIZED PUMPKIN!
SOMETHING'S WRONG.
OH GREAT! NOW THE GIRL WITH HEIGHTENED SENSES IS GONNA TELL ME HOW BAD I SMELL TOO!
BAROOOM
AAAAAHH!!
MONSTER!
I'LL TEACH YOU TO STEAL ALL MY PUMPKINS!!

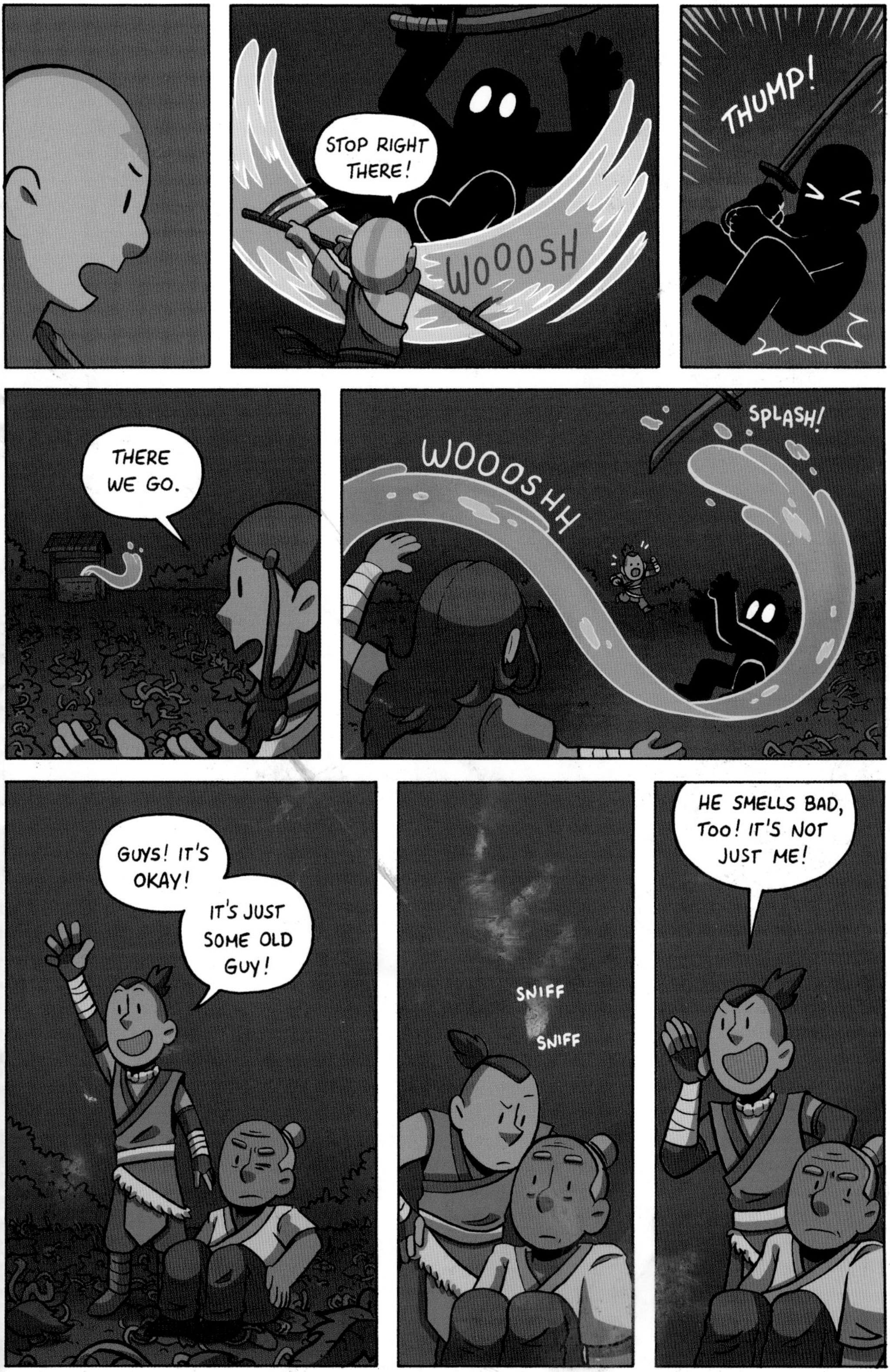
STOP RIGHT THERE!
WOOOSH
THUMP!
THERE WE GO.
WOOOSHH
SPLASH!
GUYS! IT'S OKAY!
IT'S JUST SOME OLD GUY!
SNIFF
SNIFF
HE SMELLS BAD, TOO! IT'S NOT JUST ME!

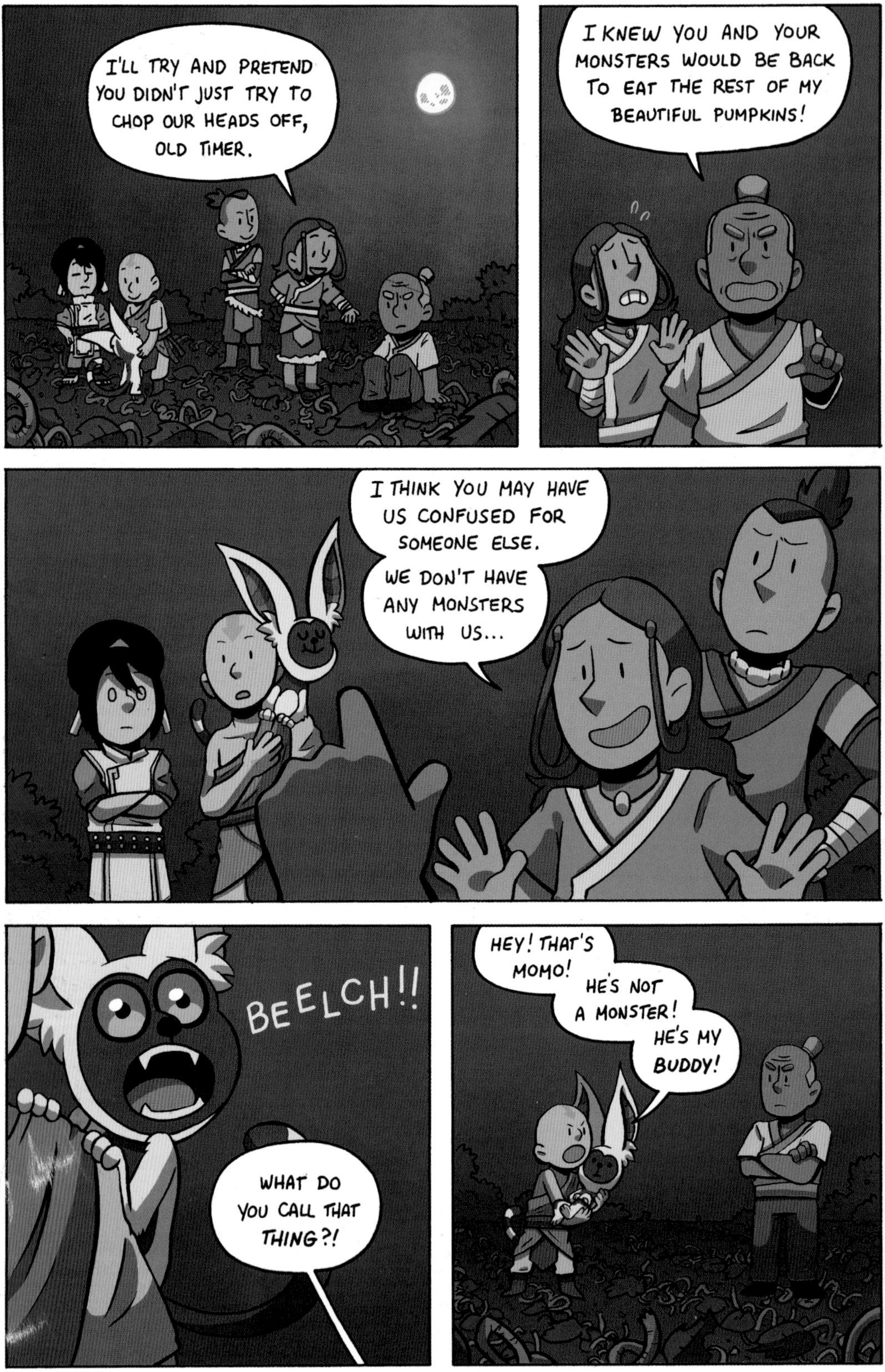
I'LL TRY AND PRETEND YOU DIDN'T JUST TRY TO CHOP OUR HEADS OFF, OLD TIMER.
I KNEW YOU AND YOUR MONSTERS WOULD BE BACK TO EAT THE REST OF MY BEAUTIFUL PUMPKINS!
I THINK YOU MAY HAVE US CONFUSED FOR SOMEONE ELSE.
WE DON'T HAVE ANY MONSTERS WITH US...
BEELCH!!
WHAT DO YOU CALL THAT THING?!
HEY! THAT'S MOMO!
HE'S NOT A MONSTER!
HE'S MY BUDDY!

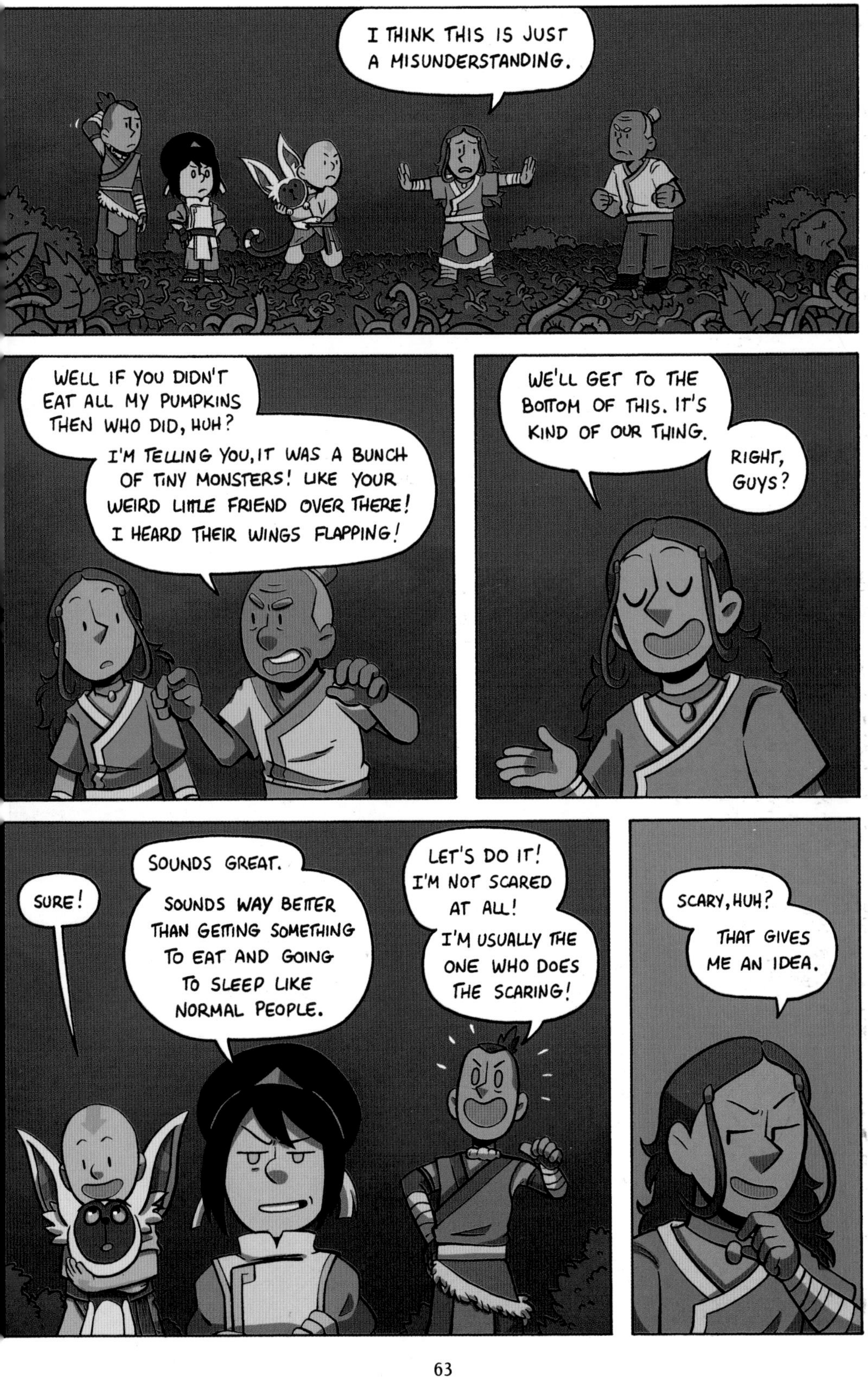
I THINK THIS IS JUST A MISUNDERSTANDING.
WELL IF YOU DIDN'T EAT ALL MY PUMPKINS THEN WHO DID, HUH?
I'M TELLING YOU, IT WAS A BUNCH OF TINY MONSTERS! LIKE YOUR WEIRD LITTLE FRIEND OVER THERE! I HEARD THEIR WINGS FLAPPING!
WE'LL GET TO THE BOTTOM OF THIS. IT'S KIND OF OUR THING.
RIGHT, GUYS?
SURE!
SOUNDS GREAT.
SOUNDS WAY BETTER THAN GETTING SOMETHING TO EAT AND GOING TO SLEEP LIKE NORMAL PEOPLE.
LET'S DO IT! I'M NOT SCARED AT ALL!
I'M USUALLY THE ONE WHO DOES THE SCARING!
SCARY, HUH?
THAT GIVES ME AN IDEA.

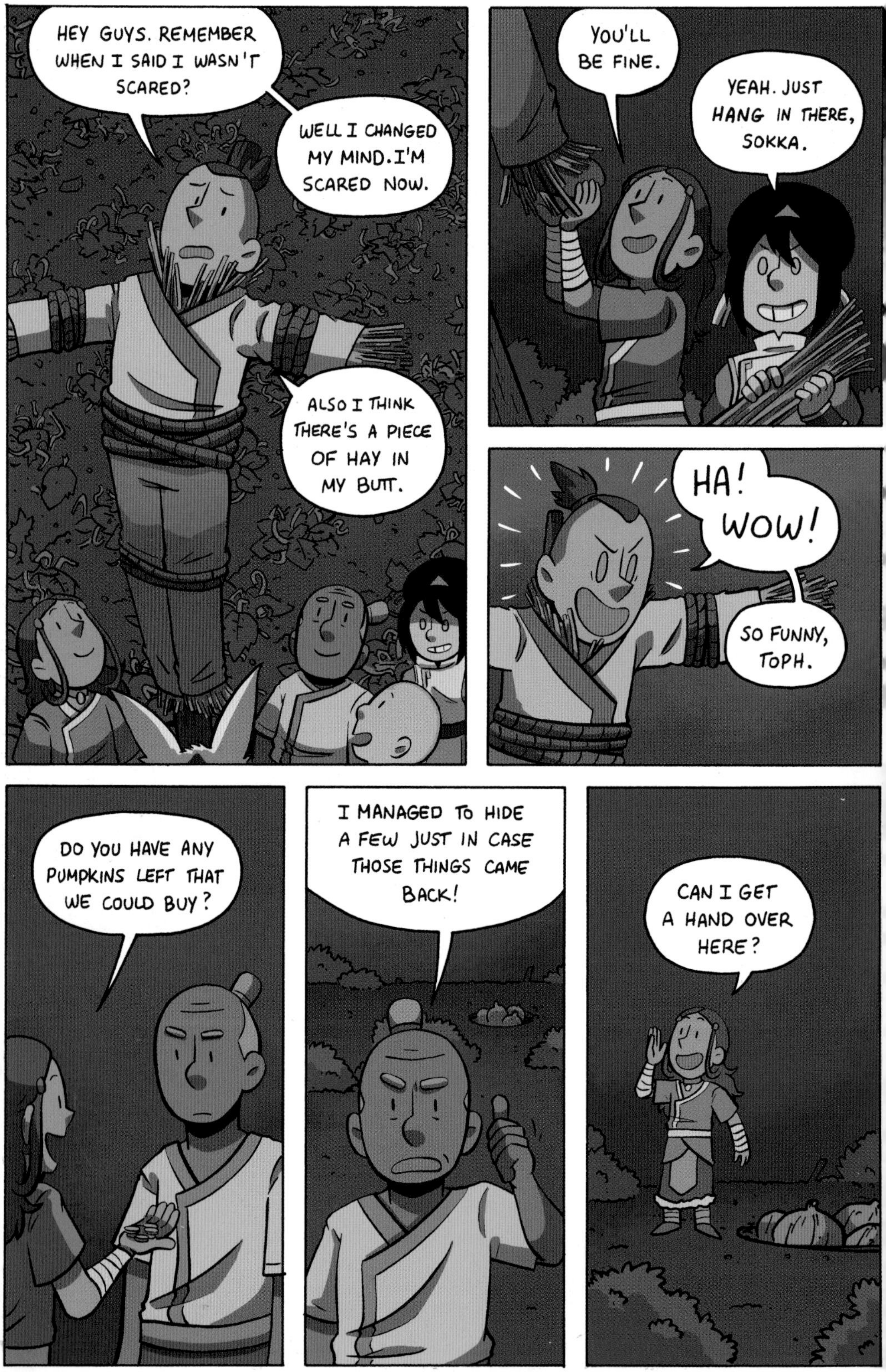
HEY GUYS. REMEMBER WHEN I SAID I WASN'T SCARED?
WELL I CHANGED MY MIND. I'M SCARED NOW.
ALSO I THINK THERE'S A PIECE OF HAY IN MY BUTT.
YOU'LL BE FINE.
YEAH. JUST HANG IN THERE, SOKKA.
HA! WOW!
SO FUNNY, TOPH.
DO YOU HAVE ANY PUMPKINS LEFT THAT WE COULD BUY?
I MANAGED TO HIDE A FEW JUST IN CASE THOSE THINGS CAME BACK!
CAN I GET A HAND OVER HERE?

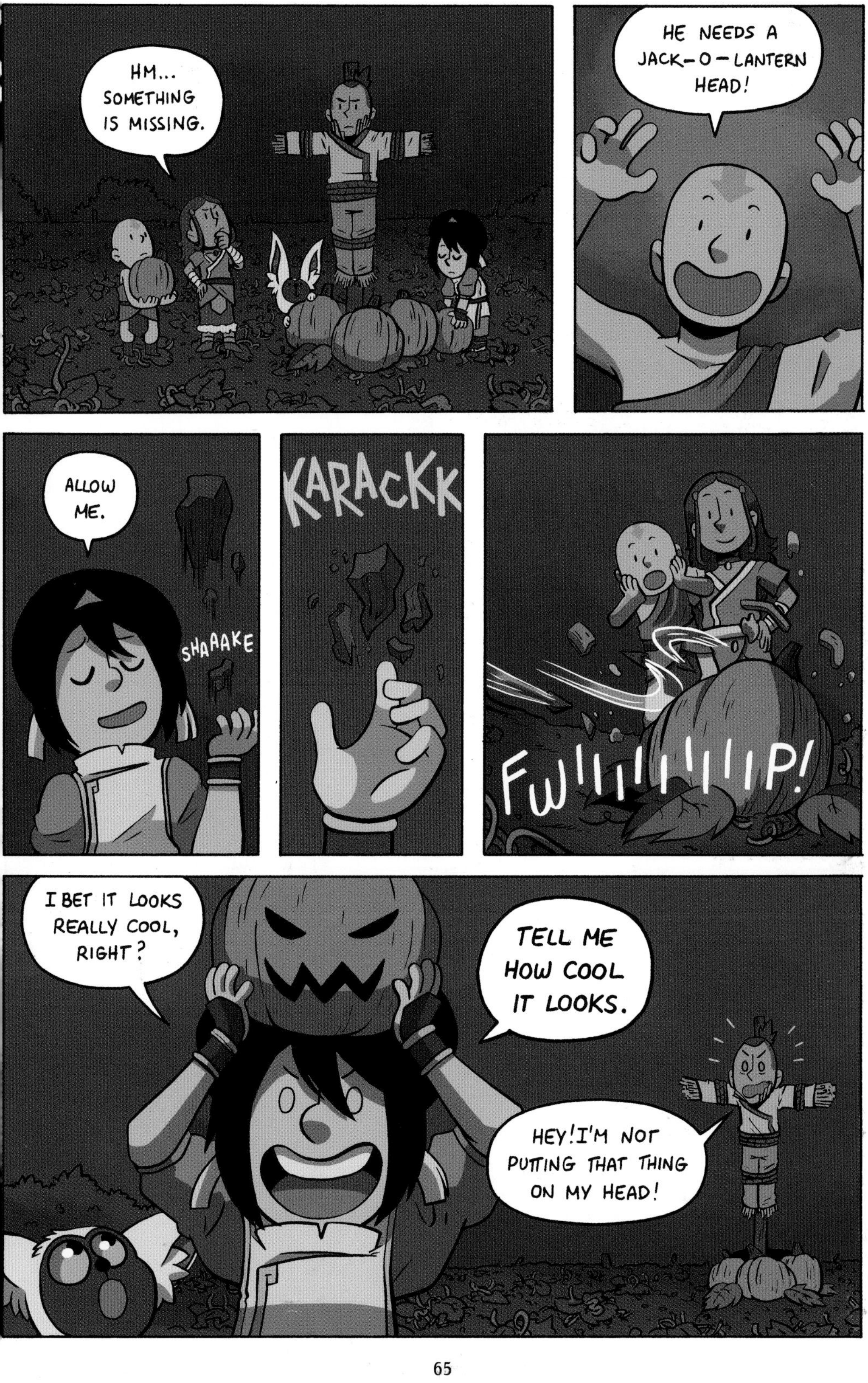
HM... SOMETHING IS MISSING.
HE NEEDS A JACK-O-LANTERN HEAD!
ALLOW ME.
SHAAAKE
KARACKK
FWIIIIIIIIIP!
I BET IT LOOKS REALLY COOL, RIGHT?
TELL ME HOW COOL IT LOOKS.
HEY! I'M NOT PUTTING THAT THING ON MY HEAD!

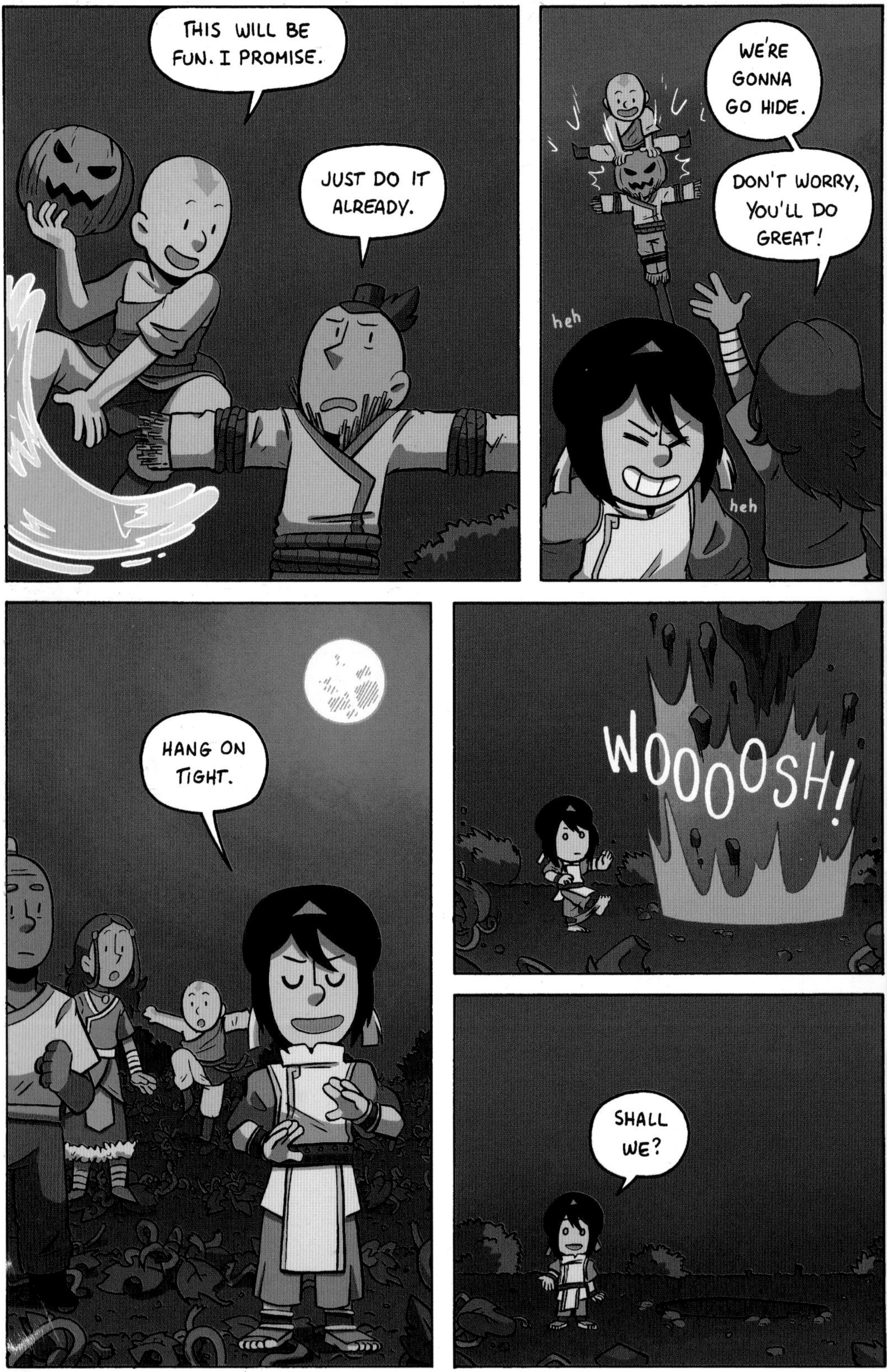
THIS WILL BE FUN. I PROMISE.
JUST DO IT ALREADY.
WE'RE GONNA GO HIDE.
DON'T WORRY, YOU'LL DO GREAT!
heh
heh
HANG ON TIGHT.
WOOOOSH!
SHALL WE?

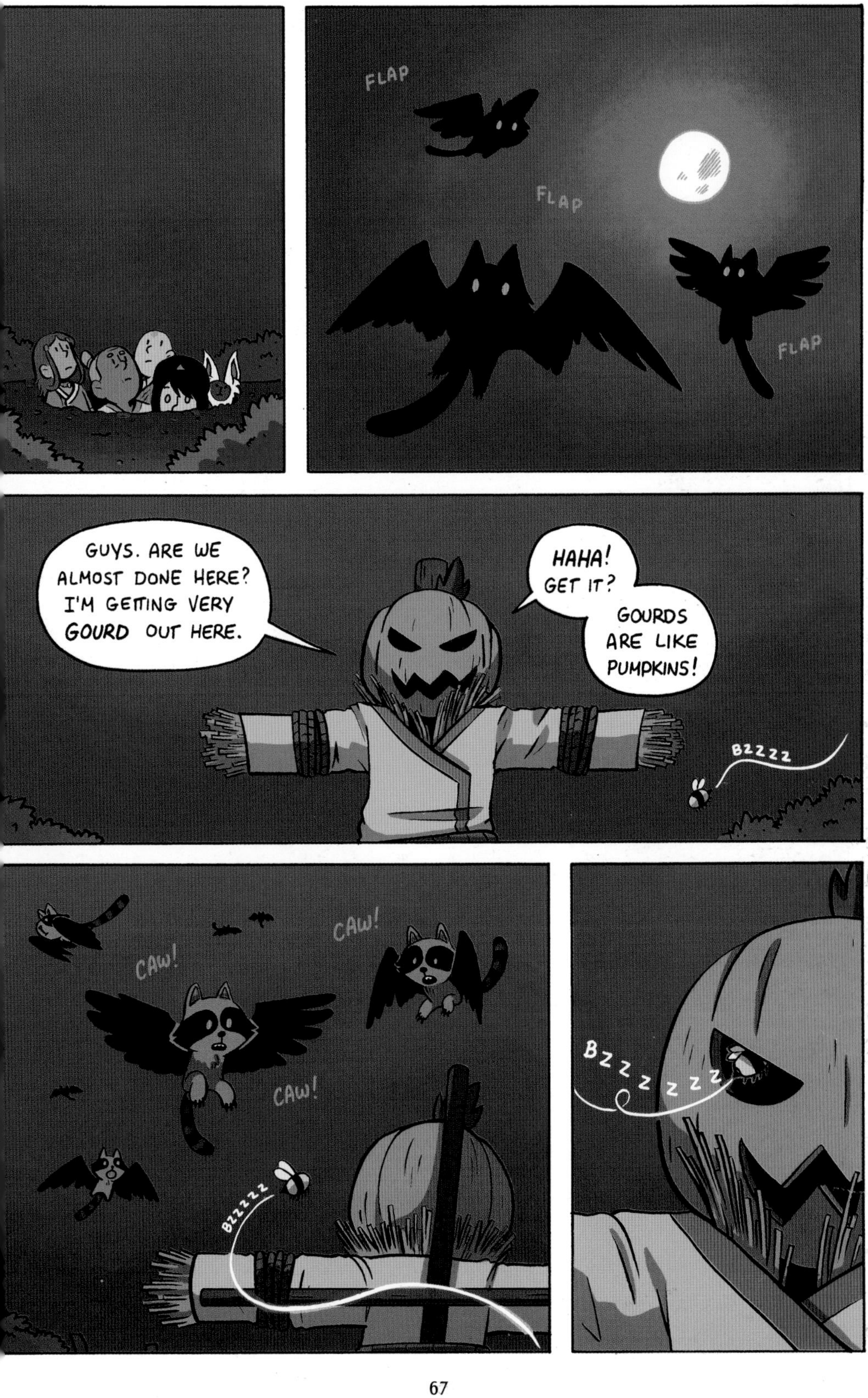
FLAP
FLAP
FLAP
GUYS. ARE WE ALMOST DONE HERE? I'M GETTING VERY GOURD OUT HERE.
HAHA! GET IT?
GOURDS ARE LIKE PUMPKINS!
BZZZZ
CAW!
CAW!
CAW!
BZZZZZ
BZZZZZZZ

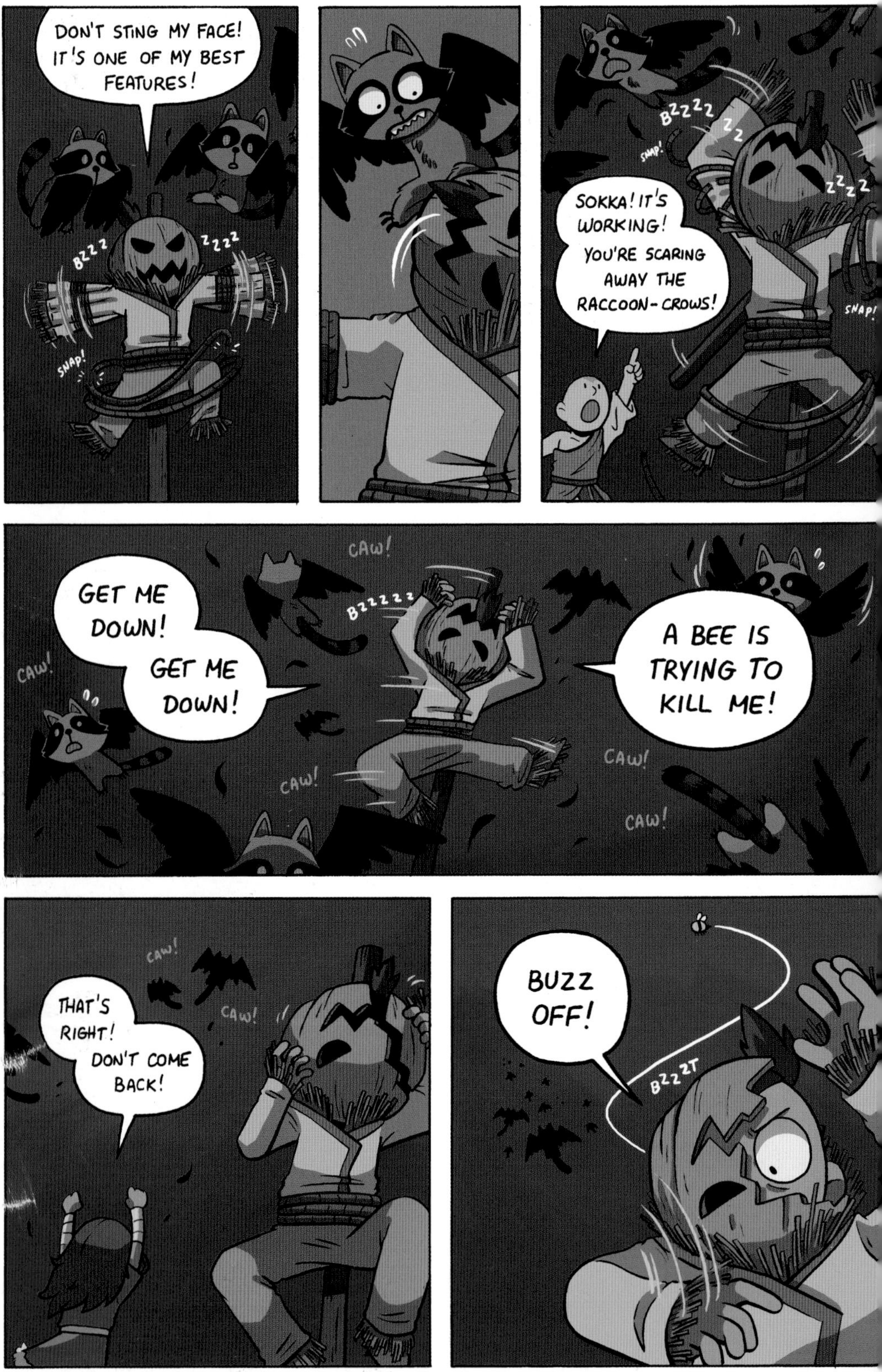
DON'T STING MY FACE! IT'S ONE OF MY BEST FEATURES!
BZZZ
ZZZZ
SNAP!
BZZZZ
ZZ
SNAP!
ZZZZ
SOKKA! IT'S WORKING! YOU'RE SCARING AWAY THE RACCOON-CROWS!
SNAP!
CAW!
BZZZZZZ
GET ME DOWN! GET ME DOWN!
A BEE IS TRYING TO KILL ME!
CAW!
CAW!
CAW!
CAW!
CAW!
CAW!
THAT'S RIGHT! DON'T COME BACK!
BUZZ OFF!
BZZZT

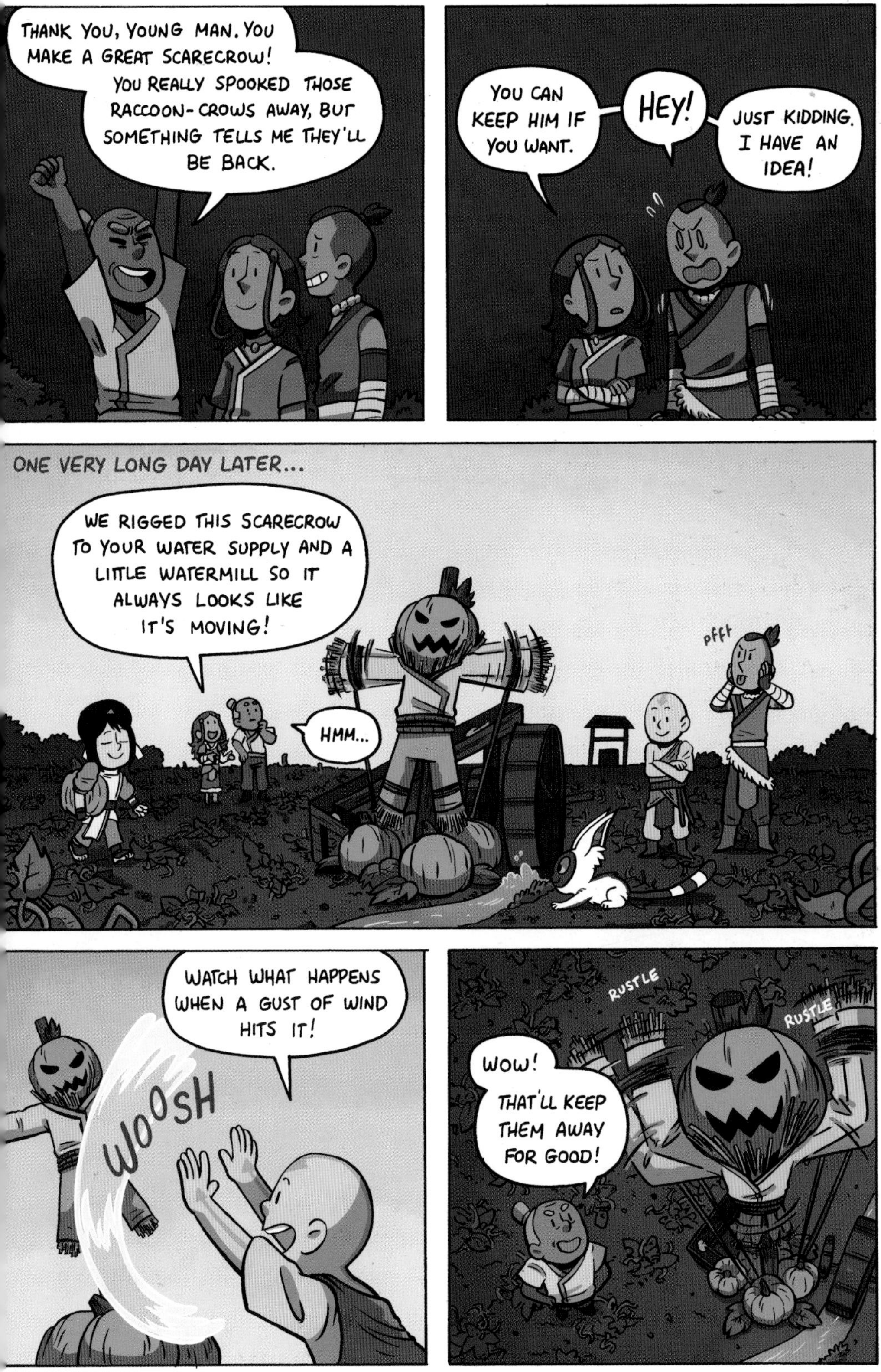
THANK YOU, YOUNG MAN. YOU MAKE A GREAT SCARECROW!
YOU REALLY SPOOKED THOSE RACCOON-CROWS AWAY, BUT SOMETHING TELLS ME THEY'LL BE BACK.
YOU CAN KEEP HIM IF YOU WANT.
HEY!
JUST KIDDING. I HAVE AN IDEA!
ONE VERY LONG DAY LATER...
WE RIGGED THIS SCARECROW TO YOUR WATER SUPPLY AND A LITTLE WATERMILL SO IT ALWAYS LOOKS LIKE IT'S MOVING!
HMM...
pfft
WATCH WHAT HAPPENS WHEN A GUST OF WIND HITS IT!
WOOSH
RUSTLE
RUSTLE
WOW!
THAT'LL KEEP THEM AWAY FOR GOOD!

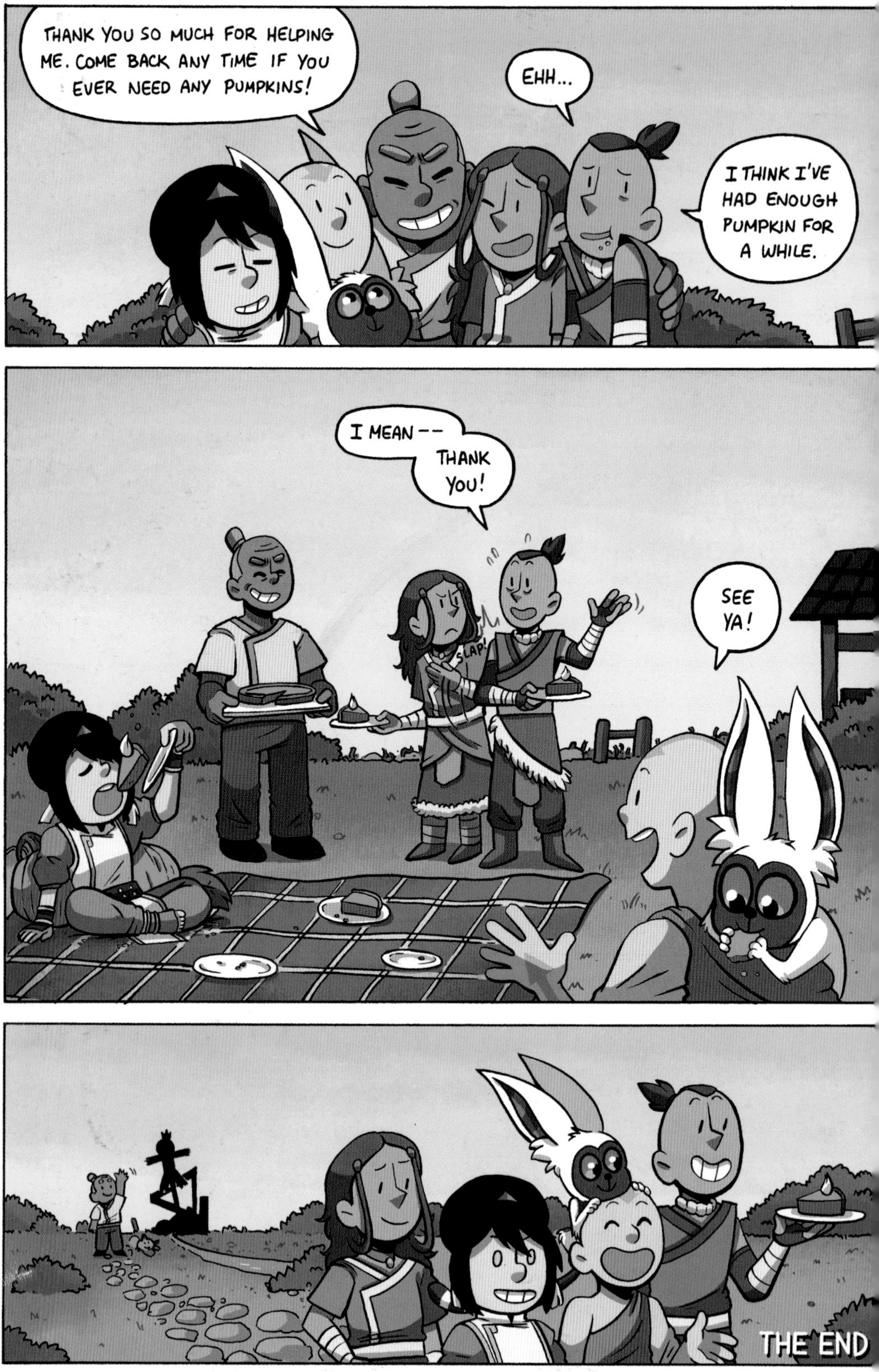
THANK YOU SO MUCH FOR HELPING ME. COME BACK ANY TIME IF YOU EVER NEED ANY PUMPKINS!
EHH...
I THINK I'VE HAD ENOUGH PUMPKIN FOR A WHILE.
I MEAN -- THANK YOU!
SLAP!
SEE YA!
THE END

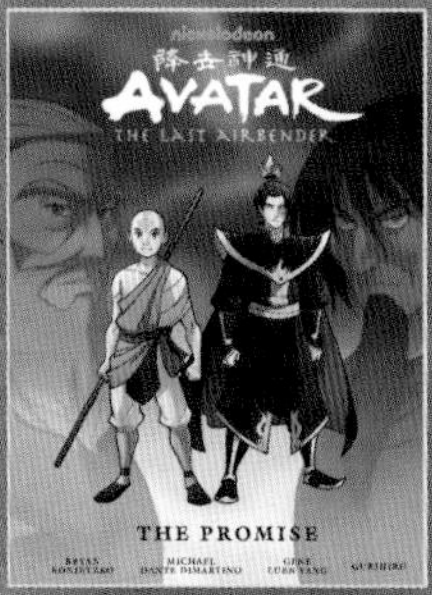
nickelodeon
AVATAR
THE LAST AIRBENDER
THE PROMISE

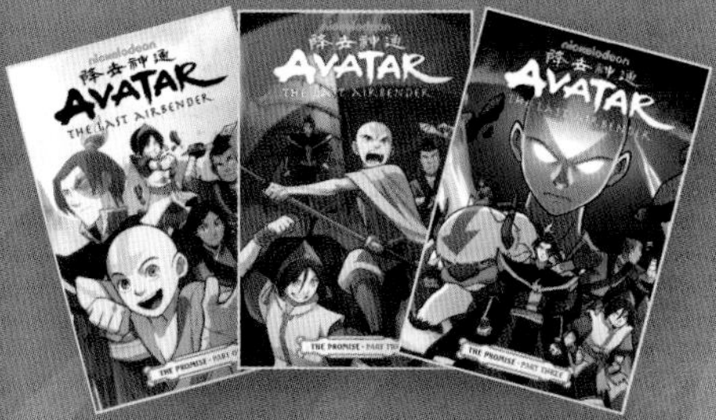
AVATAR
THE LAST AIRBENDER

Avatar: The Last Airbender—The Promise Library Edition
978-1-61655-074-5 $39.99

Avatar: The Last Airbender—The Promise Part 1
978-1-59582-811-8 $12.99

Avatar: The Last Airbender—The Promise Part 2
978-1-59582-875-0 $12.99

Avatar: The Last Airbender—The Promise Part 3
978-1-59582-941-2 $12.99

Avatar: The Last Airbender—The Search Library Edition
978-1-61655-226-8 $39.99

Avatar: The Last Airbender—The Search Part 1
978-1-61655-054-7 $12.99

Avatar: The Last Airbender—The Search Part 2
978-1-61655-190-2 $12.99

Avatar: The Last Airbender—The Search Part 3
978-1-61655-184-1 $12.99

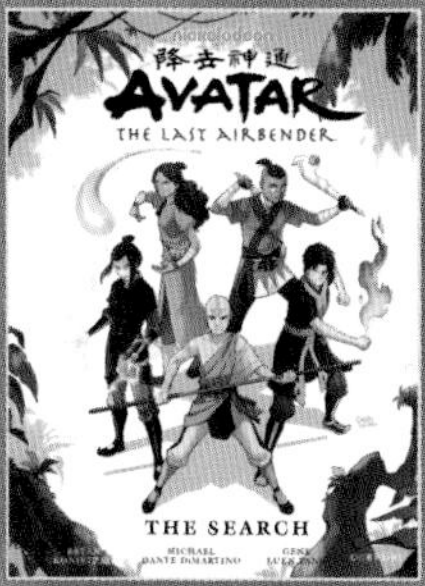
AVATAR
THE LAST AIRBENDER
THE SEARCH

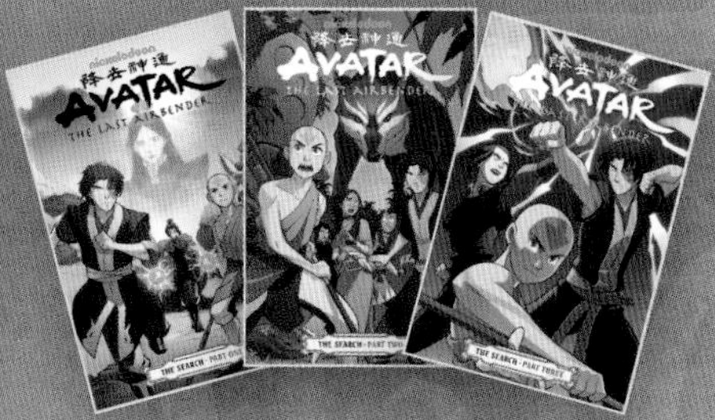
AVATAR
THE LAST AIRBENDER

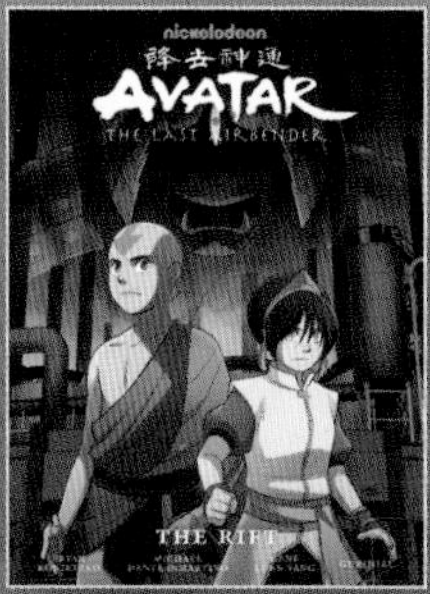
nickelodeon
AVATAR
THE LAST AIRBENDER

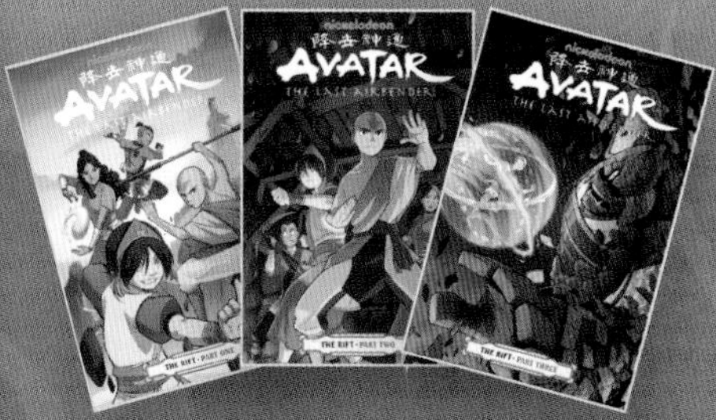
AVATAR

Avatar: The Last Airbender—The Rift Library Edition
978-1-61655-550-4 $39.99

Avatar: The Last Airbender—The Rift Part 1
978-1-61655-295-4 $12.99

Avatar: The Last Airbender—The Rift Part 2
978-1-61655-296-1 $12.99

Avatar: The Last Airbender—The Rift Part 3
978-1-61655-297-8 $10.99

Avatar: The Last Airbender—Smoke and Shadow Library Edition
978-1-50670-013-7 $39.99

Avatar: The Last Airbender—Smoke and Shadow Part 1
978-1-61655-761-4 $12.99

Avatar: The Last Airbender—Smoke and Shadow Part 2
978-1-61655-790-4 $12.99

Avatar: The Last Airbender—Smoke and Shadow Part 3
978-1-61655-838-3 $12.99

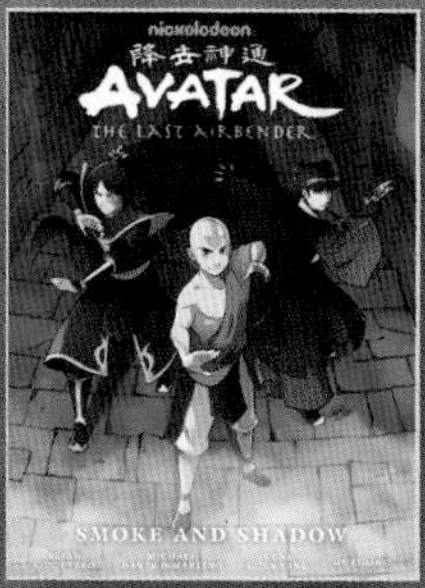
nickelodeon
AVATAR
THE LAST AIRBENDER
SMOKE AND SHADOW

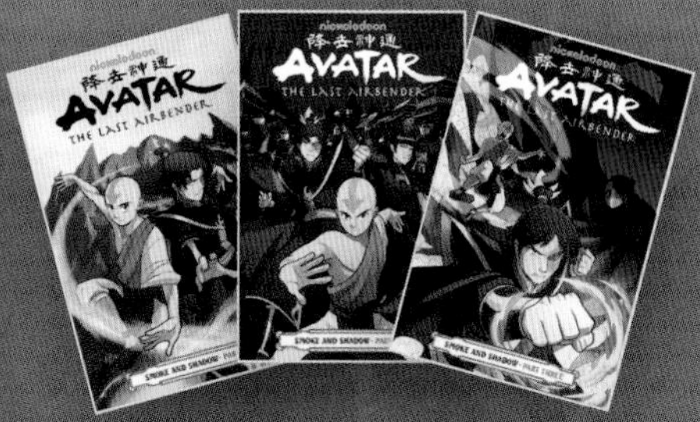
AVATAR
THE LAST AIRBENDER